SCANDALOUS PASSIONS

HIGHLAND
MÉNAGE SERIES

SCANDALOUS PASSIONS

HIGHLAND
MÉNAGE SERIES

NICOLA DAVIDSON

This book is a work of fiction. Names, characters, places, and incidents are the product of the author's imagination or are used fictitiously. Any resemblance to actual events, locales, or persons, living or dead, is coincidental.

Copyright © 2020 by Nicola Davidson. All rights reserved, including the right to reproduce, distribute, or transmit in any form or by any means. For information regarding subsidiary rights, please contact the Publisher.

Entangled Publishing, LLC
2614 South Timberline Road
Suite 105, PMB 159
Fort Collins, CO 80525
rights@entangledpublishing.com

Scorched is an imprint of Entangled Publishing, LLC.

Edited by Lydia Sharp
Cover design by Bree Archer
Cover photography by Period Images
caracterdesign, andeva, and lucentius/GettyImages

Manufactured in the United States of America

First Edition May 2020

For all those who understand and uphold these romance truths: that nothing about sex or kink, explicit language, and queer happily ever afters is modern. This is for you, with much love.

Chapter One

Stirling Castle, Scotland, July 1504

The knock at her chamber door sounded more battering ram than human. Powerful. Relentless. Deadly.

Even before the heavy oak swung open, Lady Janet Fraser knew who it was. There was only one man King James IV sent when he had reached the end of his tether with a recalcitrant courtier: Sir Lachlan Ross, his Highland Beast.

And she had been most recalcitrant, choosing to remain in the castle rather than leaving it, as the king's other former mistresses and illegitimate children had been ordered to do when he wed the young English princess Margaret Tudor.

Now Janet's day of reckoning had come. And if James had sent the Beast, he was most displeased.

"Lady," Sir Lachlan growled. "The king will see you. Now."

Janet swallowed hard as she got to her feet, forcing herself to meet the warrior's frigid brown gaze. Everything about Sir Lachlan was terrifying. She was tall for a woman, as tall as most men, but he towered over her by a full head. His shoulders were massive, his chest broad, his arms thick with muscle after many years of expertly wielding a longsword in battle, and he always wore black from hat to hose, apart from a red doublet that many whispered was refreshed in the blood of his enemies. And while his pitch-black hair reached shoulder length, as was fashionable, he always wore it tied back with a length of leather. All the better to see the scar that dissected one slashing black brow and stretched to his ear.

Terrifying.

"Will he, indeed?" she retorted, pleased when her voice quavered only a little. Even after their affair had ended and the king married her off to one of his privy councillors, he had been kind to her. When her husband passed of a fever, he had been kinder still. Surely James would show her mercy today.

Sir Lachlan scowled, one huge paw of a hand curving around her elbow. "*Now.*"

The jolt that raced through her at his impersonal touch was so startling Janet stumbled. Saints alive! Had she lost her wits? Clearly she needed a new lover in her bed if her body responded to *Lachlan Ross*. Especially when it appeared he wanted to snap her like a twig. Or heave her over the ramparts. It certainly wasn't lust darkening those fathomless eyes.

"One moment," she said just to compose herself. "I need to...hook up the train of my gown."

Surprisingly, Sir Lachlan released her and stepped back, granting permission with a curt nod. Yet even as she bent down to gather up an armful of dark-blue velvet, she could feel his eyes burning into her, and it made her usually dexterous fingers clumsy. When at last she had finally conquered that task, adjusted her gable hood so it sat straighter on her head, and smoothed the wide fur-lined cuffs at her wrists, she again met his gaze.

"There. You may escort me to see the king," Janet announced crisply. "Is he receiving many this afternoon? They are not long arrived from Linlithgow; I thought he and the queen might have tarried there longer. I'm sure she prefers Linlithgow to Stirling Castle."

"No."

Janet hesitated, forcing a laugh. "No? To which point?"

Sir Lachlan's lips tightened, and he took her elbow again, leading her across the comfortably furnished chamber and out into the torch-lit hallway. Even in summer the stone walls and floor held a cool dampness, and the row of torches sitting in their small wrought-iron cradles were a welcome source of light and warmth.

"Only you," he said. "And Lady Marjorie Hepburn."

Confusion furrowed her brow. She well knew what her own sins were, but it was hard to imagine Lady Marjorie's—the king's beautiful young ward had only recently been released from imprisonment in a remote convent. Allegedly for her comfort and protection, but as Lady Marjorie's father, Lord Hepburn, had been involved in the death of the king's father at Sauchieburn back in 1488, it was hard to see it as anything other than punishment.

"Oh."

"Fret not, lady. No harm will befall you. I swear."

Janet almost stumbled again. As soon as she returned to her chamber, she would throw those almond-paste comfits out the window. Bad enough the sweet treat had caused her to feel lust at the Highland Beast's touch, but now she'd heard a faint note of *tenderness* in his tone?

Impossible.

Thoroughly unnerved, she remained silent for the rest of their walk across the inner close. While Stirling Castle had stood for centuries, a brooch that fastened the Highlands and Lowlands together, James had made several improvements. The two newest buildings were the King's House, where he entertained privately and listened to petitions, and the jaw-droppingly magnificent Great Hall.

The King's House had three principal rooms; on the ground floor there was a hall, where visitors and petitioners waited, and a great chamber for favored noblemen. However, up a turnpike staircase was his private chamber, where only his closest friends and advisers were permitted. This was their destination, and all those watching enviously knew it. Few had unfettered access to the king, but this day Janet would gladly decline the honor and return to her book of poetry.

How angry would James be at her disobedience? In what way would he punish her? Hopefully not banishment to a convent. Virginal Lady Marjorie might have survived years in one, but Scotland's most notorious sinner wouldn't last an hour.

At the foot of the stairs, two armed guards waited. One inclined his head. "Sir Lachlan. Lady Janet. The king awaits you."

How she hated these stairs. Whether climbing or descending, the spiral made her dizzy, and the walls always seemed to press in on her. Oddly, with her escort behind her, she felt a trifle safer. Another armed guard opened the door at the top with a polite bow and ushered them into the lavishly furnished chamber.

"Lady Janet," greeted the king, his cool formality unnerving her further.

"Your Grace," she murmured, sinking into a deep curtsy.

James Stewart wasn't a tall man or especially broad shouldered, but his fashionable, fiercely intelligent presence filled a room. Visitors were often lulled by his easy charm, humor, and gift for languages, but those shrewd brown eyes missed nothing. He'd won several decisive victories on the battlefield and lured back many Scottish nobles who had abandoned the court in disgust because the previous king had disastrously surrounded himself with advisers who were tailors and masons.

"False meekness from my fiery lass is unbecoming," he continued sharply. "Look at me and explain why you disobeyed my order. Do you know the trouble you've caused me? The queen is in a lather."

Janet bit her tongue, lest she comment on the tiresome lathers of a fourteen-year-old queen. The king had wed for duty, not love, and an unhappy wife could mean trouble with England. "Forgive me. I meant no disrespect to Her Grace."

Her former lover sighed. "King Henry has at last sent Margaret's second dowry installment. And money for her expenses. She and her retinue of English ladies are damned expensive…I cannot afford any unpleasantness. Our peace treaty is uneasy at best."

"Your Grace—"

"You must leave, Jannie," said James, his temper easing to familiar affection. "I've sent away all my mistresses. All my bairns. It claws my soul, but such is the burden of a king with an unsteady crown."

Her shoulders slumped. To be forced to leave Stirling Castle, the only place that had ever truly felt like home, was a crushing blow. "When?"

James took her hands and squeezed them, smiling sadly even as his relief shone through at her acquiescence. "Tomorrow, beloved."

So soon! Plainly, he would not be turned or teased in this matter. Rejection by the king, her former lover and dear friend, hurt more than words could express.

"Where must I go?"

"I am granting you land near St. Andrews. Fresh air,

excellent hunting. I shall visit when I can. Sir Lachlan will escort you there and keep you safe henceforth."

Janet froze.

What?

• • •

Sir Lachlan will escort you there. And keep you safe henceforth.

The king's words had the impact of a boulder into a pond, so startling that Lachlan could scarcely comprehend them.

In one breath, he'd been granted his dearest wish—to be close to Lady Janet Fraser, the woman who dominated every lusty dream he'd ever had—but also forced to face his worst fear: sent from the king's side, a position of favor he'd held for seventeen years.

His early childhood had been pleasant enough; his bold, strong, and affectionate mother was the cherished mistress of a laird. But one winter day, they'd been out walking, and a raiding party from a rival clan had knocked him unconscious and taken her. Days later, her body was recovered, and all light disappeared from his life. With his mother gone and his father inconsolable and turning on him, his half brothers took the opportunity to show him a disdain and resentment that became crueler as the years passed.

Until he grew and began to best them in fights, of course.

Then his father had taken notice and started training him with longsword, pike, mace, and dagger. At just thirteen summers, he'd fought his first battle—against that rival clan. His father had been killed, but they'd won a decisive victory, and important men had taken note of Lachlan's size and skill. Mere weeks later he'd been brought to court to serve as a guard and companion to then Prince James. They had done everything together: fought battles the length and breadth of

Scotland, bedded comely wenches, drank taverns dry. James had ensured Lachlan mastered French and Latin, and he in turn helped James with Gaelic so he might converse easier with those in the Highlands.

But now…his king—his close friend—was sending him away.

Lachlan squared his shoulders against the harsh and unexpected blow. Yet he couldn't remain silent. Or stoic. Not in regard to this.

"Your Grace," he began, taking a breath to slow his words, lest he humiliate himself in front of Lady Janet. The king knew of his longstanding and most wretched speech affliction—how he deliberately spoke in short, clipped sentences to manage it—and now waited patiently for his question. "You wish me…to stay at St. Andrews?"

James glanced over at Lady Janet. "Will you excuse us a moment, Jannie?"

The redheaded beauty stared back at him, her green eyes blazing with hurt, but she eventually curtsied and retreated to the sun-warmed window seat to give them some privacy.

"My fiery lass is unhappy with me," said James with a rueful smile as he absently pulled his purple-velvet ermine-lined mantle tighter about his shoulders. "But she'll soon see 'tis for the best."

"I did not think," replied Lachlan carefully, not wanting to offend the king, "that you would send me t-to protect Lady Janet in her new home. Have I d-displeased you?"

"No! The very opposite. I ask this boon because you are the only man in Scotland I dare trust with the task. Yet I confess, Jannie is but one half of it. She does not know it yet, but I am awarding her guardianship of Lady Marjorie Hepburn until I decide on a husband for the lass. So you see, I am placing not one but *two* precious jewels in your care. Because I know you will not mistreat or hold them captive for your own ends but protect them with your life."

Lachlan nodded. Everyone knew of the king's affection for Lady Janet, and his ward was quite a marriage prize, despite her unfortunate father. Men would commit devilish acts to command women far less valuable than these. But while he could see it pained the king to send the three of them away, James was a practical man. Queen Margaret did not appreciate beautiful unwed Highland ladies at court, and the king had a peace treaty with England to maintain.

"And Lady Janet?" Lachlan asked. "Is she to be m-married also?"

"I wager not. Jannie has expressed no desire to wed again, for she loved Master Fraser well. Besides. She is a woman of thirty-three summers, and barren. Men want a younger wife who can give them heirs," said the king with a shrug almost cruel in its dismissiveness.

Lachlan barely suppressed a snort. Maybe noblemen or those with a crown did, but even after thirty summers, he felt no great urge for a family. A tall flame-haired wife with a saucy tongue and plentiful spirit...well, that was a different matter entirely. Not even on his deathbed would he confess the lewd, forbidden thoughts he had about Lady Janet most nights. Those slender, bejeweled fingers tangling in his hair as she pressed his face between her thighs. Her long legs straddling him as she rode him hard. Her pouty lips wrapped around his cock or whispering wicked demands in his ear.

Alas, the chance of having such a highborn, intelligent beauty in his bed was as likely as the sun rising in the west. Lady Janet had been the king's mistress and then wed Fergus Fraser, a privy councillor and learned scholar who'd studied ancient manuscripts and even practiced alchemy. Who had written verse as fine as William Dunbar's.

A worthy man.

Far better than a landless knight with little means and

only his sword arm to offer. In truth, Lachlan was still unused to hearing *Sir* before his name. He had climbed high for a bastard son, and there were those who hated him for it. None had dared to challenge him as yet, but he remained ever watchful, ever ready to slay an enemy. He was the king's Highland Beast, after all.

"Of course, Your Grace. Many heirs," Lachlan muttered eventually, wanting to kick himself for his poor conversation. James had never once mocked his speech or his lack of learning, but it was hard to feel anything other than inadequate in front of someone so gifted. The king could speak on any topic, with any man, even change language from one sentence to the next. He was equally comfortable with envoys from foreign lands as he was breaking bread with a lowly crofter. It was how he'd taken a realm torn apart with lawlessness, deceit, and divided loyalties after his father's disastrous reign and slowly, painstakingly began to sew it back together.

James smiled and clapped him on the shoulder. "You'll go with my blessing and friendship. And a bag of gold. Do not think for a moment I am ungrateful for your service and loyalty. No one has been a better companion, and as I said, I would trust no other with this task. Have you met the Lady Marjorie?"

"I have not."

But I am curious about this young woman—imprisoned most of her life—whom I must protect. Is she plotting revenge? Broken of soul? Excessively pious? Something else entirely?

"Virgin still," James explained, "but a buxom little beauty made for long nights in bed. If Margaret were not here…"

Lachlan almost smiled as James sighed irritably and leaned against a cloth-covered oak table. The king's gifts were not limited to matters of state. He could charm the birds from the trees, and many a fair maiden had happily surrendered her virtue to him. James loved women. All women. If his young English queen expected fidelity, she would be sorely disappointed, but at this time she had thwarted his romantic plans.

"Have you told Lady Marjorie of her fate?" Lachlan asked.

"Not yet. But soon…ah, here she is now," said James, as the heavy chamber door swung open.

Lachlan turned. And almost forgot to breathe.

For there stood a beautiful young woman, brown haired and petite, wearing a modest linen gown that in no way disguised what must be the plumpest, most luscious curves in Scotland. About as different from tall, slender, flame-haired Lady Janet as possible and yet equally as alluring.

He would be guarding both.

Strictly forbidden from either.

God's blood. Purgatory on earth, indeed.

...

King James was the last man she wanted to see this day. Yet as ever in her life, she had no say in the matter.

Lady Marjorie Hepburn nodded at the guard who held the chamber door open for her, an opportunity to pause and catch her breath after hauling her plump form up the stairs at great pace to escape the condemning gazes and sneers below. She'd been a fool to think Stirling Castle would be different from imprisonment in the cold, bleak, and lonely convent. There might be men here, the rooms finely furnished, and the clothing fashionable, but she was still unwanted. Still blamed for something her late father had done. Still the young girl she'd once been, yearning for a kind word, an affectionate touch, even one person to love her…and finding none.

The dream that had sustained her in the convent—how

exciting and magical life would be at court—had dwindled now. She had found no freedom behind these ancient stone walls; no laughter or new friends to confide in; no gentle, chivalrous knight to kiss her hand or recite poetry. As ward of the king and existing entirely at his pleasure and mercy, the most she could hope for was a Scottish husband of means who wouldn't beat her and was young and healthy enough to give her the children she'd always wanted. As a mother, with sons and daughters to lavish affection on, she might at long last find purpose alongside that other elusive emotion: happiness.

The king smiled. "Lady Marjorie, I bid you welcome. Forgive me for not seeing you sooner, but I had a great many matters of state to attend to."

His tone was affable, but as he moved toward her, she could hear a clinking sound, and her heart sank. The convent prioress's cold warning had been true. James did wear an iron chain of penance under his doublet, in sorrow over his father's death. Like the courtiers downstairs, he would never forget the high treason Lord Hepburn had been party to.

"Your Grace," she whispered, curtsying deeply. "It is an…an honor to be here."

"Your chamber is comfortable?"

"It is lovely. The tapestries are beautiful."

"Good, good. There is someone I wish you to meet," said the king, gesturing to his right.

"Of course…" Marjorie's voice trailed off as her mouth abruptly forgot how to form words.

She was being introduced to Lady Janet Fraser? One of the most influential women in Scotland?

That would be a mark of favor, surely.

Confusion turned her mind to mud, but there was no mistaking the stunning beauty now standing in front of her. That blazing-red hair, not quite constrained by a simple hood. Wide green eyes the color of fresh moss. Creamy skin. Unusually tall, enviably slender, wearing a fashionable blue velvet gown with wide fur-lined cuffs, beautifully embroidered sleeves, and a jeweled girdle around her waist. Even at the convent, they'd heard of Fiery Janet, albeit as a stern cautionary tale on the terrible vice of lust. She had been the king's mistress for several years, and the pair had half scandalized, half delighted the realm with their public displays of affection and heated arguments. The prioress had called her the worst sinner in Scotland. She hadn't mentioned how utterly compelling Lady Janet was, though, or how her rosy pink lips invited the lewdest of thoughts.

How do you kiss, lady? Soft and sweet, gentle as the petals of a rose? Or do you take command, teasing and nipping and plundering until your lover whimpers with need?

The other woman cocked her head, frowning a little, and for one dreadful moment, Marjorie thought she'd said the words aloud. How could she think such a shocking, forbidden thing? Ladies did not have sinful thoughts about other ladies. But then the redhead turned to the king and lightly rested her hand on his sleeve.

"This is Lady Marjorie, Your Grace?" she said.

James inclined his head. "Indeed. Lady Marjorie, may I present my most beloved friend, Lady Janet Fraser. A widow, scholar, healer, and a woman of means."

"Uh…a pleasure—a *great pleasure*—to, er, meet you, my lady," Marjorie said, awkward in her eagerness to make the acquaintance of this bold, beautiful woman, the one person in the realm who might withhold judgment on her. "How very accomplished you are."

"His Grace flatters me overmuch. I suspect there is a reason," said the older woman wryly.

James shifted a little. "Not at all, beloved. But I have a most wonderful surprise for you both."

Now Lady Janet looked wary, and Marjorie stepped back and twisted her fingers together. This did not sound like the king was about to gift them a trinket or offer them a place at the top table during tonight's feast in the Great Hall.

"A surprise, Your Grace?" Marjorie asked through bone-dry lips. If he meant to send her to another convent, she would flee in the dead of night and take her chances with beasts, brigands, and warring clans. Even the thought of being imprisoned again was unbearable; unlike the nuns, she took no joy or comfort in silent contemplation, poverty, and chastity.

James smiled. "Indeed. Until I decide on a husband for you, Lady Janet is to be your new guardian. You will leave Stirling together on the morrow to live with her at her estate in St. Andrews."

The startling news made her breath hitch. Once again a decision had been made with no care for her wishes…and yet for the first time, she welcomed it. To live in the country with Fiery Janet herself! While she had little knowledge of the other woman's character or how she treated servants, it was hard to believe she would oversee a somber household. This woman was bold and learned. Forthright in speech. Experienced in the ways of men.

"As it pleases Your Grace," Marjorie murmured, unable to quell the flickering of that wretched flame of hope inside her. Even a short time in the companionship of this woman might be the best of her life.

Lady Janet looked thoughtful. "The king's champion, Sir Lachlan Ross, will escort and protect us both."

"*The Highland Beast?*"

"Some say, lady," growled a voice to her left.

Marjorie nearly jumped a foot. Sir Lachlan had moved silently yet was enormous. Even in her innocence of men, he was obviously dangerous. Deadly. His hands rested behind his back in a nonthreatening manner as he inclined his head, but those dark-brown eyes seared straight into her soul, and the ruby-studded hilt of a sheathed dagger glowed at his hip. By the saints, any moment now she would begin confessing all her secrets.

Somehow she managed a curtsy. But she couldn't speak; she could only stare at this dark, craggy mountain masquerading as a courtier. No doubt they all considered him rough and raw. Uncivilized. Yet she couldn't stop her thirsty gaze drinking him in. Would his hands be calloused? Was his massive chest as hard as it looked? How would *he* kiss?

Swallowing hard, Marjorie attempted to regather her scattered wits. The Highland Beast and Fiery Janet, darkest night and brightest day, watching over her. Guiding her.

Pleasuring her?

She shuddered, her nipples hardening against the bodice of her unadorned gray velvet gown at the shockingly wayward thought. *No.* She was a grown woman of twenty-two summers, who well knew such miracles did not happen. Not for her would there be strong arms to hold her tightly and long kisses to make her burn. Nor would there be love.

But there might be conversation. Even friendship.

And that was more, so much more, than she'd ever had.

Chapter Two

Never did he feel more uncomfortable, unlearned, or baseborn than at a feast in the Great Hall.

Lachlan hesitated at the door, resisting the urge to cross himself before entering. But the building inspired cathedral-like reverence. Beyond the fact it was new—only finished the previous year—and the largest hall in Scotland, it was just so...wondrous. The outside had been coated in lime wash, and the golden glow could be seen for miles around. There were many pairs of tall windows, some with stained glass, and heating came from not one but *five* fireplaces. At the far end was a raised dais where the king, queen, and important guests sat. They had their own table and each sat on their own carved chair. Everyone else sat on benches at two long trestle tables covered in a white cloth, which were moved away after the feast for dancing and pageants. Above where he stood now was the gallery where the minstrels played.

Truly the jewel of Stirling Castle.

"Sir Lachlan," said an amused voice behind him, "you are far too competent masquerading as a door. Do allow us inside."

Heat flashed along his cheekbones at Lady Janet's teasing words, but when she placed her hand on his back and attempted to nudge him, he almost moaned. Had anyone else tried such an act, they would have found themselves short a hand. Or at least with several broken fingers. With her, he wanted to stay still just so she would touch him again.

But that wasn't what she wanted. And his mind and body had settled humiliatingly quickly into comfort at obeying her commands.

Even if they weren't the commands he truly desired.

Squaring his shoulders, Lachlan marched on. All around him were French and English dignitaries, privy councillors, nobles and their wives, even a few clan lairds seated at the long trestle tables. The noise had already reached deafening levels as conversation battled harp and flute to be heard.

"Wine, Sir Lachlan?"

He inclined his head at the servant, gesturing for him to fill Lady Janet's and Lady Marjorie's goblets before his own. Then he took a long, fortifying swallow. Plenty would be needed to assist in managing his speech in the presence of two beautiful ladies. Hell. What if they wished to dance later on? His feet might move with the lightness of angel wings on the battlefield, but add in a floor and music, and they became hewn stone.

"Do you know where we are to sit, Sir Lachlan?" asked Lady Marjorie, and he turned again to see her sky-blue eyes wide and complexion pale as she glanced around.

"Aye, lady," he replied as gently as he could to reassure her, when on most days, his voice sounded like chains being dragged through purgatory. He wasn't named Beast for his size alone. "Just follow me."

"May I...may I take your arm?"

Lachlan blinked at the timid request. He would never

be a true courtier; his stone feet, rough voice, and ugly face put paid to that. If he attempted to pick a rose with his paw hands, he yanked out the entire bush, and with his affliction, he would never be able to recite verses of poetry. But for some utterly unknown reason, he found himself offering his left arm to the tiny but mouthwateringly lush Lady Marjorie, and her shy smile warmed a part of him he'd thought frozen forever.

Then he hesitated, looking uncertainly at Lady Janet. Even the thought of offending her…

"Do not fret," she said archly, her green eyes gleaming as she parroted his words from earlier in the day. "I shall walk beside you but not take your sword arm. Or touch your dagger. Unless you ask me *very* nicely."

Lachlan's breath caught, but before he could reply, she turned to greet a nobleman and his wife. Probably a good thing. Of course she hadn't meant anything wicked by her words. That was a thousand nights of lusty dreams about Lady Janet trying to trick him.

Shaking his head at his own foolishness, he moved forward, then adjusted his stride so Lady Marjorie wouldn't trip on the hem of her gown. She had changed from the gray to one of leaf green; it had a low square bodice that lovingly cupped her ample breasts and hips, silver thread–embroidered sleeves, and a simple silver girdle about her waist.

"Pretty," he blurted.

"Beg pardon?"

Lachlan groaned inwardly. It would be far better if he didn't speak at all for the rest of the feast, but Lady Marjorie looked at him expectantly. "Your gown."

"Oh! Oh, thank you. It's my best, if rather unfashionable compared to other gowns. I love the color; it reminds me of leaves after rainfall. And I did the embroidery myself. I enjoy it. Maybe the only thing I liked about convent life—ample time to sew."

He nodded as the words tumbled from her lips like a rushing river, and she gripped his sleeve a little tighter. It seemed Lady Marjorie was equally uncomfortable in the Great Hall; understandable when, like him, she was an outsider resented by most of those present. Utterly unjust, when—like his low birth—her father's treasonous act could not be changed.

A short trumpet burst saved him from having to say anything further, and gasps went up around the hall as two servants carried out a silver tray with a rampant unicorn sculpted of spun sugar. This meant the first course would be served presently, so he ushered the two ladies to the front of the royal dais, where he bowed and they curtsied to James and Margaret. Then they sat near the end of the cloth-covered trestle table to the right of the dais, the position of highest favor. Thankfully velvet cushions had been tied to the wooden bench; without them it would have been a hard endurance for arses large and small.

As much as the Great Hall remained too grand for his blood, it stung to know this would be his last feast in the king's presence for a long while. He would miss James. Their pilgrimages to the four corners of Scotland, the bloodthirsty battles they had fought side by side, the thrill of defeating enemies and then enjoying the spoils of victory. And yet... the thought of hunts rather than war, a large feather bed with thick quilts in a warm chamber rather than a hard pallet in a corner, wasn't entirely unappealing. Nor was protecting the two most beautiful women in Scotland—one pure fire, bold and brazen and fierce; the other spring rain, soothing and gentle and refreshing.

He'd lived for years with unrequited lust and tender feelings for Lady Janet. But something stirred within for Lady Marjorie as well, and the notion unsettled him.

Really, he needed to keep distance from them both.
If only to retain his own sanity.

. . .

After a lifetime of plain convent food, the countless trays carried out by a small army of servants made her dizzy.

Marjorie tried not to make owl eyes at the colorful, heavenly-scented array, but it was nigh on impossible. Whole chickens, duck, geese, swans, even fully dressed peacocks. Haunches of beef and venison, boars' heads with apples in their mouths, pies, jellies, and several kinds of cooked vegetables. Her stomach rumbled, and she licked her lips and stared down at the pewter plate sitting in front of her, lest anyone see how ravenously hungry she was. The bread and butter with small ale she'd had at sunrise seemed a thousand years ago now.

With admirable efficiency, the servants placed a selection of the dishes into the large stale-bread trencher sitting halfway between her and the man sitting to her left. Lady Janet and Sir Lachlan would share one, but unfortunately she had to eat with a stranger.

"You're the Hepburn lass," said the well-dressed man, glaring at her, his gray-flecked beard twitching in affront. "Bad blood."

"*Sir*," she began, but he'd already rudely turned away. Nor did he ask what she might like to sample from their shared trencher before carefully using his eating knife to cut slices of meat and a spoon for vegetables and other soft dishes, as was proper and clean.

No, he was using his *hands*.

Her stomach rebelled at the sight of fingers trailing through sauce and handling meat, and Marjorie pressed her fingertips to her mouth.

"Not hungry, lady?"

She glanced to her right at Sir Lachlan's words and watched in envy as he wielded his ruby-hilted dagger with precision to cut choice slices of venison for Lady Janet and place them on her plate.

"N-no," she whispered miserably as, of course, her stomach chose that moment to gurgle like a thunderclap.

Sir Lachlan stared at her, his thick black brows drawing ominously together. "You lie."

Marjorie bit her lip. This close, the Beast looked even darker and more fearsome, and she could only see Lady Janet if she leaned well forward or back. Yet her hunger pains had clearly addled her mind, for even more than before, she wanted to touch him. Stroke that jagged scar on his face. Smooth his hair. Even answer him honestly.

Taking a deep breath for courage, she tugged on Sir Lachlan's sleeve so he might lean down. "The man said I had bad blood. And used his hands in the trencher. He touched *everything*. I don't think he wishes to share with me. See... like he's doing now."

"Wait, lady."

In one surprisingly graceful movement, he stood and stepped back over the bench. A moment later, there was a muffled choking sound, and the stranger was no longer sitting beside her but hanging in midair.

By the saints, Sir Lachlan had him by the throat!

Gasping, Marjorie looked left and right, utterly unsure of what to do. People farther along the bench were still eating and talking. Did this happen often? Should she say something? Summon help?

"Sir Lachlan!" boomed a voice from the dais. "Lord Kerr is turning as red as your doublet. What is his crime?"

"Poor manners, Your Grace," replied the Beast, shaking the man as though he weighed no more than a feather.

King James nodded. "I see. Best remove him from my Hall, then. I'll only have guests who know how to behave. Do set him on his feet, though."

Sir Lachlan actually scowled but allowed the drooling, shaking man to leave, which he did at great pace. Just as swiftly, a servant removed the spoiled trencher. Now others at the table were watching her, some from across the room as well. A few were laughing and pointing, but most were censorious. Queen Margaret's stony gaze expressed pure dislike.

Marjorie's stomach rumbled again, and she fought the urge to weep. The sooner she could leave Stirling Castle, the better.

"Choose, lady."

Startled, she looked up to see Sir Lachlan gesturing at a refreshed trencher being held by two smiling servants.

He had arranged food for her. After removing the man who had been so ill mannered, albeit rather violently.

"Ah, anything, r-really," stammered Marjorie, her mind still trying to piece together what had just happened. "Whatever is easiest."

"What do you *wish*?" he asked.

And there it was—the question she had waited her whole life to hear. Not from family or a friend but a man she had met mere hours before.

"Swiftly, my dear," said Lady Janet with a mischievous grin, as she held up her wine goblet to be refilled. "Sir Lachlan will carve for you. His hands may look like bear paws, but they are astonishingly nimble. A skill welcome in more than one room of the castle, I wager."

Was the Beast…*blushing*?

Although she didn't quite understand what Lady Janet meant, it did sound rather naughty, and Marjorie fought the urge to giggle. Never would she forget her first, and probably only, feast in this Great Hall. "I should like chicken, a little venison, and a slice of beef pie. And some of that pottage with the carrot and leeks. A pear. Oh, and a few almond pastries too…"

Her voice trailed off, and her own cheeks heated at such gluttony. The prioress would have given her several lashes for this. But Lady Janet merely nodded and pointed out the dishes for Sir Lachlan to take a sample from. Soon her pewter plate was full and her wine goblet replenished.

When he sat down again, Marjorie leaned close. "Thank you, Sir Lachlan."

He nodded, not meeting her eyes. "Lady."

"No, I mean…thank you for everything. For helping me," she said softly, placing her hand over his and gently squeezing.

By the saints, his hand was warm. So large, hers almost looked childlike on top of it. But as she'd thought, it was rough with slight calluses, and when his hand jerked a little, those calluses rubbed her fingertips. Tingles raced through her body, oddly centering in that forbidden place between her thighs, and she shifted uncomfortably on her cushion.

Knowing how sinful it was, Marjorie had never dared to touch herself there. But sometimes in bed at night, she'd cup her breasts and rub her thumbs across her nipples until they were taut. Never for long enough, though; to be caught risked great punishment.

What would those huge calloused hands feel like on her breasts? Unlike her, Sir Lachlan would have no trouble cupping them. And he would rub and rub…

A soft moan escaped her lips.

"Eat, lady," Sir Lachlan growled, and she nearly fainted in embarrassment. Silly Marjorie Hepburn, so desperate for touch she'd been stroking the knight's hand as though he were a fractious horse.

Her face hot enough to boil water, Marjorie took a gulp

of wine, then used her small eating knife to spear a slice of chicken. The other man had been banished from the Hall for poor manners, but hers weren't much better.

It was definitely time to leave Stirling Castle.

• • •

Her last feast here had been memorable, at least.

Janet sighed and finished her wine. Sir Lachlan turning full Beast on the hapless Lord Kerr aside, the food had been splendid and the jesters amusing. Once they finished eating, the trestle tables had been cleared away, the minstrels had struck up a merry pipe tune, and James gallantly led Margaret to the floor to begin the dancing. Even the queen's usually dull and proper ladies joined in, and the Great Hall had been alive with the sound of hands clapping, heels stomping, and breathless laughter as they danced until their feet ached.

She and Lady Marjorie had both tried to coax Sir Lachlan away from the wall, but he'd adamantly refused. Fortunately others had been eager to partner her—lords, lairds, and foreign dignitaries, all swarming in. Of course, they wanted more than dancing. Many had made blunt offers; it was known throughout Scotland she was a lusty woman. Oddly, though, none tempted her.

Usually during a feast, she would cast her eye over the men—not the married ones, for she preferred a tranquil life free of angry wives—make her choice, then spend the rest of the evening in bed. Back when they'd been lovers, James had always visited her chamber after a feast. Once wed, she'd spent many splendidly debauched evenings with her dear departed Fergus. On this night, though, it seemed she would sleep alone. If that wasn't irritating enough, she had downed several goblets of the delicious red wine, and as James and Fergus both would have attested, wine provoked her to unearthly heights of wickedness.

"Are you unwell, lady?" Sir Lachlan asked.

On another day the low rasp in her ear might have been startling, but comfortably mellow, she began to shake her head at him. Then halted.

Maybe her evening could be saved after all.

"I fear so," she lied. "Would you escort me to my chamber? Lady Marjorie is speaking to the king and queen, so will be quite safe."

He hesitated before nodding. "Aye."

Moments later, they stepped outside. After the cloying stench of sweat, grease, food, burning wood, and wilted flowers, the cool, fresher air was most welcome, and Janet inhaled heavily as she glanced over to the oldest part of the castle where her chamber was located. Unlike the other royal castles, Stirling had little accommodation for guests. James might have more pressing reasons to send her away, but he wouldn't be dismayed to have another chamber to make use of.

As they walked across the inner close, her heel caught on an uneven stone, and she stumbled. But with the reflexes of a cat rather than the bear he reminded her of, Sir Lachlan curled one hand under her elbow and halted a fall.

There…those wretched tingles again.

Her heart pounding, Janet tilted her head and studied him. "I find you…intriguing," she murmured.

"Oh? How so?"

"You say very little yet see everything. The king trusts you above all, but you have no family. No wife. I know you and James have rutted your way through the realm, yet unlike him, you have no bairns. You choke an ill-mannered man at a table, would kill an enemy with nary a blink, but are kind to a friendless convent orphan. Although in truth, that isn't a hardship. Lady Marjorie is rather delicious, is she not?"

Sir Lachlan glanced down at her, true surprise on his face. "Er..."

"Oh, come now. God creates beauty in many forms; all must be appreciated. And you liked it when she stroked your hand, yes?"

He didn't reply, but his fingers flexed on her arm. A resounding yes from the Beast.

"I shall counsel you not to bed the king's virgin ward under his nose," Janet continued merrily, the wine making her reckless as he led her up the stone steps and into a wide torch-lit hallway.

"I would not!" he growled. "I mean...no virgins. I like... experience."

Janet blinked. Well. This stoic, taciturn Highlander would offer a little something when pushed. "Then I must beg forgiveness, stealing you away from your current mistress. I wager she awaits you, naked and wet and aching to be plundered."

Sir Lachlan sucked in a harsh breath. "Your ch-chamber, lady."

"So it is," she said, leaning against the heavy oak door. "Do you know, on nights like this I miss my husband most. He knew wine unleashed wickedness in me. Made me especially demanding..."

There was a long, long silence. But her escort didn't move. Then, he gritted out, "It does?"

Janet closed her eyes in sweet remembrance. "Oh yes. See, our marriage was different than most; in the bedchamber, he ceded total command. Certain men love to receive instruction. They *crave* it. I would make him kneel and pleasure me with his tongue and fingers, and only when I was thoroughly sated would I permit his release. He spent so hard when I rode him, bucking like a spring colt as he gave me every drop of his seed..."

The silence stretched again. Inwardly cursing her wine-loosened lips, Janet opened her eyes and looked up.

Except it wasn't scorn or disgust on Sir Lachlan's face. Just pure *yearning*.

But how could that be? He was the Highland Beast!

Shocked to the core, Janet could only stare as his face became impassive as hewn rock. Had her eyes deceived her? Then she glanced down to see a huge bulge jutting against his hose and doublet.

"My, my," she purred, reaching out but deliberately halting her hand an inch from his engorged cock. "So wonderfully thick. And in urgent need of stroking. If you were just a little closer..."

Sir Lachlan's fists clenched, his chest rising and falling with unsteady breaths. Then, with a guttural sound he stepped forward, thrusting his cock hard against her palm. "*Yes*."

Greedily, her fingers closed around him, squeezing and rubbing through his hose.

He moaned.

"Oh, you like that?" Janet teased, excited beyond belief at the thought of this magnificent column of flesh buried deep in her needy cunt after he had pleasured her senseless. "I may allow you in my chamber. But I have rules. *Unbreakable* rules."

His hips jerked, shoving his cock even harder against her hand. "*Please*. Let me kneel. Whatever you wish."

"Very well—"

"Sir Lachlan!"

They both froze at the guard's hail from the end of the hallway.

"What?" snarled Janet.

"Beg pardon, my lady, but the king asked for Sir Lachlan. At once."

She would boil James in oil. Dismember him with a rusty spoon. Just because he chose not to bed his young wife, everyone else must sleep alone also?

Damn his eyes.

Sir Lachlan stepped back with a wince before adjusting his cloak to hide the evidence of their near interlude. "Lady Janet," he said quietly, bowing. Then he marched away.

Furious, she stormed into the chamber and latched the door behind her. Right now she wanted to hurl something breakable at the wall. Like the king. Yet for the first time, she was thankful they were leaving for St. Andrews. James could keep his lonely bed at Stirling; at her new estate, it would be another world entirely. A world where Janet Fraser ruled supreme.

Next time there would be no interruptions.

Only pleasure.

Chapter Three

On the road to St. Andrews, near Loch Leven

Traveling—even leisurely and in relative comfort—became torturous after a full day, and despite years of accompanying the king or her husband, she would never grow used to it.

Janet stifled a wince, her bones aching from being jolted up and down and side to side on the rocky, uneven track masquerading as a road. For safety, rather than riding, James had insisted on a sturdy wooden wagon pulled by two horses. The wagon was spacious enough: there was room for their trunks; the baskets of food, wine, and small ale provided by the kitchens at Stirling Castle; and small sections of the leather cover could be rolled up to allow in fresh air. They also had velvet cushions to sit on and furs for warmth. Yet she envied Sir Lachlan, who was outside on horseback, enjoying not only the crisp air and sun on his back but also a far easier journey as his mighty warhorse disdainfully sidestepped the rocks and holes the wagon hit with great precision.

Lady Marjorie suffered worse, though. Unused to wagon

travel, she'd spent most of the journey gripping the wooden bench, her color somewhere between moss and snow. She'd not napped at all and had only managed a few bites when they'd briefly stopped for a meal of bread, cheese, cold sliced beef, dried fruit, and pastries.

Her beautiful new ward just looked so…lost. Lonely. Again, Janet mentally berated James for a poor decision. Women being punished for the sins of their fathers, brothers, or husbands made her blood boil. Lady Marjorie's long imprisonment at the convent had only increased her guilt in the eyes of the court, but she'd been a lass of *six* when the old king was murdered. Hardly party to events.

Bah. Foolish and unjust.

Suppressing her irritation, Janet instead smiled sympathetically at Lady Marjorie. "How are you feeling?"

Her ward tried to smile in return and failed utterly. "A little better."

"I shall warn you now, my dear, lying is not something I tolerate. I must insist upon the plainspoken truth. When I ask you how you feel, I do indeed wish to know."

"Oh. I…uh…" Lady Marjorie blinked, her bewilderment clear.

Saints alive. Has no one ever cared about her?

"I think you are aware," Janet began, gentling her usually brisk tone, "that I am no prioress or prison guard. I believe the king placed you in my care as an apology of sorts, fully aware that I oversee…hmm…a less structured household. So you might be comfortable, have companionship, and learn the ways of a wife in preparation for your future marriage."

"The ways of a wife?" said Lady Marjorie, her eyes brightening for the first time since the start of the journey. "You mean intimate matters…the plainspoken truth?"

Janet's lips twitched. "I cannot expect it without providing it. So yes, I would explain wifely duties. With enough detail to curl your toes, because knowledge is power, and young women are all too often kept ignorant. That is what you want, yes?"

Her ward nodded eagerly, her blue eyes shining with such hope that Janet's heart clenched a little. That Lady Marjorie could still feel such emotion after her long imprisonment was a miracle in itself. In truth there were places in the Highlands so bleak, so isolated, that not even travelers wished to tarry long. But to live in such a place for sixteen *years*...

How different her own life had been. Mistress to the king, a blissful but too-short marriage, adventures, feasts and entertainment, debating law and learning with indulgent scholars, all the court influence she might wish for...simply because she'd been caught bedding a woman.

Aileen. Her first love.

Just one long ago summer, but unforgettable. The days where she'd first discovered a fondness for dominating a lover; the power of touch and withholding or granting pleasure; of wicked words; the sweetness of soft lips, taut nipples, and dripping cunt. After they'd been caught, Aileen was hastily wed and sent away. Her own father wanted her locked in a convent, but Mother, infinitely wiser and more practical, arranged for her to go to court and meet the young and infamously lusty King James. The king graciously received his *gift* and in turn showed her family great favor. While he'd always maintained control in the bedchamber, and his wandering cock irritated her to no end, James had been a good lover. Generous. Affectionate.

Occasionally she wondered what life might have been like if her affair with Aileen had continued. Would it have eventually ended? Or would they be living together somewhere as dearest *friends*? There were so many questions left unanswered, and she'd not seen Aileen since that fateful day. Nor had she been tempted by another woman since.

Until Lady Marjorie.

Sweet and innocent yet eager to learn. Ready to be conquered yet forbidden.

"How did you bear it?" Janet asked abruptly, pressing her thighs together to ease the burgeoning ache in her cunt. "Imprisonment in a convent, I mean."

Lady Marjorie stared at her hands. "I had no choice. And I can't remember much of life before it. My mother died when I was three, my father was always at court, and I had no brothers or sisters. But…"

"Tell me. Plainspoken truth," she reminded. "And may I add, while I love the king dearly, you'll not hear defense of his decision from me. It was wrong."

"The convent always felt wrong," replied Lady Marjorie hoarsely. "It wasn't my home. I was an unwanted guest, just as I was at Stirling Castle. I never had a choice about anything—not what I wore or ate or how I spent my time. There were a great many women, but I was always alone. They wanted to be there, to serve God in a certain way, but I've never felt the calling to be a nun. I know the king will choose my husband, but at least as a wife, I will have a say in certain matters. Even a little say…"

Janet bit her lip so she wouldn't launch a tirade. Lady Marjorie had been taught to expect naught but crumbs from the table, to be grateful for them, even. And she'd had her spirit crushed. Well. She would find new direction at St. Andrews. A new beginning. "I swear, my dear, you shall have choices under my guardianship. And learn a great many things before you wed."

"Thank you. May I ask…did you choose your husband? That is, if you wish to share such a personal matter," her ward finished awkwardly.

"I did not choose Fergus Fraser. The king selected him after our long affair ended. But it was an inspired choice, and that is why you must not give up hope for a happy marriage. The king is a practical man but also a romantic at heart."

"You loved Master Fraser? Really loved him?"

Janet closed her eyes briefly against the stab of pain. "I did. I miss him a great deal. He was such a scholar, always reading. And as a privy councillor, he shared the best court chatter. I heard the scandals before most—although in fairness, I caused many of them. My unruly temper or sinful boldness."

Lady Marjorie gasped. "He did not beat you for that?"

"Saints alive, no. He wasn't that sort of man. Just a gentle soul with a talented tongue and nimble fingers that did not tire."

"*What?*"

Janet laughed. "Forgive me; that was far too bawdy for virgin ears. I have no desire to disgust or frighten you."

"I'm not," her ward denied quickly. "Just surprised... and curious. I know it's sinful to be, but it feels like I've been standing outside in the cold forever, and at last the door has opened. Please tell me. *Please.* I don't have anyone else to ask. And we're in a wagon. Sir Lachlan rides ahead, and the driver won't hear. Do you mean he kissed you? Touched you?"

"Lady Marjorie—"

"Just Marjorie. I mean, if you like."

Janet nodded. "Very well. Then I'm just Janet. To answer your question, yes he kissed and touched me. Everywhere I desired. I always enjoyed my neck being massaged, but my favorite times were when he sucked my nipples and stroked between my legs until I coated his fingers in honey...oh dear. Your cheeks are as red as my gown. Should I stop?"

"No," whispered Marjorie, squirming on her seat, her nipples now visibly pressing against the bodice of her gray gown. "Please don't stop."

· · ·

This was wicked talk. The most scandalous of conversations.

Yet after a taste, Marjorie wanted so much more. To know all the secrets of love. Right here in the covered wagon that shielded her and Janet from the world like a cocoon, and right now before the king decided on her husband and yanked her away. This was not the day for retreat back to that little girl whose life had been governed by strict rules and the chime of bells but to try and become the woman she so wanted to be: one who made her own decisions and marched forth with great courage.

"Please don't stop," Marjorie said again, her inability to sit still nothing to do with the rocking, jolting wagon. Her body felt strange, like her gown was a full size too small, her breasts sensitive, her skin warm and prickling.

Janet smiled and leaned back against her seat. "I won't. Prepare yourself, my dear."

Her guardian was just so sensual. As Janet had taken off her hood to travel, her unbound hair fell to the small of her back like liquid flames. Her green eyes were glittering, and the red velvet gown with silver embroidery she wore had tucked up around one slender thigh, offering a glimpse of stocking and satin garter. Would her skin be as soft to touch as it looked? Was the bush between her legs the same hue as her hair?

Swallowing hard against the shamefully lewd thoughts, Marjorie forced a smile. "I'm ready."

"Hmm. Where was I? Oh yes. An ode to being stroked between my legs. I often bring myself to release when alone, but it really is quite delicious when a lover does it. Do you touch yourself? I daresay you must. A body has needs."

She blushed. "I...ah..."

Janet frowned. "*Marjorie*. Never say you've been denying

yourself that."

"It's sinful," she protested weakly. "The punishment was ten lashes."

"Bah. If you don't know your own body, what you like and dislike, how can you guide a husband? They must be instructed kindly but firmly, so when it is time for bed, it is something you delight in, not dread. An ill-prepared woman is one who will feel pain. Besides. If God did not intend for women to feel pleasure, He would not have furnished us with our own special little pearl."

"Our what?"

Again, that husky laugh echoed in the wagon. "Pleasure pearl. That small bud between your legs with no other purpose than making you feel good. Forget everything else; this is all the evidence required that God truly loves us."

Marjorie blinked in confusion. "I don't...I don't know what you speak of. I've only touched my breasts. Nowhere else. Apart from bathing, but that was too swift to feel anything."

"That must be remedied at once."

Excitement flared, so strong Marjorie almost whimpered. "You mean..."

"I mean," said Janet, her eyes darkening to emerald as she flicked her lips with the tip of her tongue, "if you wish, I shall offer instruction on how to touch yourself and gain release."

"Yes! Er...yes, please. I would like that."

"Well then, my eager little student, raise your gown so we might begin."

Marjorie gripped the folds of her kirtle and gown, which were once cream colored but now more gray tinged after frequent wearing and sponging...then stilled. If she raised them, Janet would see her bare thighs. They weren't long and sleek and smooth but short, plump, and dimpled. Not to mention her rounded, fleshy belly. Would Janet be dismayed like the prioress and nuns had been, always advising Marjorie to fast, to work harder in the gardens, to walk another circle of the convent?

"I must warn you," she said miserably. "I am—"

"Delicious. Curved and ripe," replied Janet softly. "The way your hips sway and breasts bounce…I am envious. Dale to your hill. But whether we are tall and slender or petite and plump, we are all worthy of love, respect, and *hours* of tongue appreciation. Now, be a good lass and lift that gown."

Marjorie shuddered, both soothed and stirred by the kind but unmistakable command, the avid interest in Janet's gaze. "Very well."

Slowly, awkwardly, she gathered all layers of fabric and lifted them to her knees, then higher, as heat scorched across her cheekbones. How difficult this was.

"Spread your thighs, my dear," said Janet gently. "At once."

Taking a deep breath, she obeyed, and cool air ruffled the thick tangle of brown curls covering her mound. A new scent teased her senses, and she wrinkled her nose at the unusual spiced muskiness of it.

Oh no. The scent came from down there.

Embarrassed, Marjorie glanced up at Janet. Yet there was no dismay or disgust there, only smiling approval. "What should I do now?"

"Stroke yourself. Feel how soft your inner thighs are."

But her hands remained attached to her gown, seemingly unable to break free from the hold of convent life. "I can't," she choked out, bracing herself for a scolding.

Instead, Janet nodded sympathetically. "You think I don't understand what is swirling around that pretty little head of yours, but I do. Years of enforced shame. Of being told your body wasn't beautiful and needed to be corrected.

Of being denied what it craved. This first time, it might be easier if I showed rather than told you."

Marjorie's eyes widened. "You would touch me? Guide my hand?"

"If you wish. Come and sit in front of me."

As if in a dream, she moved across the swaying wagon and settled herself between Janet's splayed thighs, her head resting on Janet's shoulder. It was the strangest thing in the world sitting so close to another woman, her back pressed hard against breasts, her body encircled by another. And yet it felt wonderful. She'd never felt so warm and safe. So cared for. More importantly, she'd *chosen* to do this.

Marjorie held out her right hand, and Janet covered it with her own. Then her guardian gently pushed both down between Marjorie's legs, gliding back and forth along her inner thigh, brushing the crisp hair between her legs but not parting it.

A soft whimper escaped her lips, and her hips jerked, trying to force touch to her aching mound.

Janet tsked. "Naughty."

"Are…are you going to strap me?"

"Quite unnecessary. I shall simply withhold pleasure until you behave."

Marjorie shuddered at the murmured words that tickled her ear. "I'll be good."

"Delighted to hear it."

Soon Janet guided their hands down again, parting her nether curls and teasing her most secret flesh with feather-light strokes. The sweet torment made her pant, but she'd learned her lesson and neither closed her thighs nor thrust her mound higher. Her reward was a caress to her slick, petal-soft folds, and the briefest nudge of a spot so sensitive she cried out.

"Is that…?"

"It is indeed your pearl. Small but sensitive and craving affection."

"Like me," Marjorie replied with an unsteady giggle. "I…ooooh…"

How can anything feel so good?

Their fingertips were slick with musky wetness, and now Janet guided them to surround Marjorie's swollen pearl. Circling. Rubbing. Unable to stop herself, she rocked her mound against their interlaced fingers, desperate for ease. As if she understood, Janet applied firmer pressure with the heel of her hand, forcing Marjorie's fingers to cup her mound and shallowly penetrate her entrance with a fingertip.

Sounds escaped her mouth, raw and wild. Something was happening inside of her, something overwhelming that would change her forever. A part of her resisted, thrashing in an attempt to escape the intense sensation, while the rest begged for more.

"No, do not fight it," said Janet harshly, holding her firmly. "You are going to be a good lass and spend for me. I want to hear your pleasure. Feel every spasm of that sweet virgin cunt."

At the wicked words, a mighty wave of sensation began at her core and flowed outward with a rush. Barely able to muffle the scream that tore from her throat, Marjorie surrendered helplessly to her first release.

Eventually she slumped back against Janet's chest, shaking.

"Shhh, there now," Janet crooned, smoothing her hair. "How did that feel?"

"I don't even know how to describe it. Like I swooned. Or soared. Maybe both," she replied, knowing she'd sinned—with another woman, at that—yet too befuddled in the aftermath of intense pleasure, the sheer delight of being held and touched, to care.

"Let me—"

Something thudded into the side of the wagon, and they both froze. A heartbeat later, an arrowhead pierced the leather cover, and as Marjorie shrieked in fear, Janet shoved her onto the wagon floor before protectively covering her.

"Wh-what is happening?" she asked as icy terror gripped her, a stark contrast to the heat of moments before. Was it a raiding party? They could have no better champion than Sir Lachlan, but he was one man. Their driver was no warrior.

Janet didn't lie. "The wagon is under attack."

. . .

Never had Lachlan felt such ferocious rage, such pure bloodlust, as he did right now.

Lady Janet and Lady Marjorie had been *threatened*. But whoever these raiders were, they would never succeed. They would not abduct or hurt the ladies under his protection. He wasn't a child, a frightened little boy who could be knocked aside now. He was the Highland Beast, the king's champion, a hardened warrior who had killed countless men in battle. And in his current state of unrequited love and unsated lust for Lady Janet, the additional swirling confusion around his attraction to Lady Marjorie, he positively ached for a fight.

Lachlan unfastened his mantle and slid from his saddle, his longsword thumping against his thigh as he hit the ground. Storm, his pitch-black mount, nickered softly and pawed the ground. Eager, just like his rider.

"Guard the wagon," he snarled at the ashen-faced driver, who nodded, dagger already in hand.

Then his gaze roamed the line of trees. The snap of twigs under feet and flashes of black and brown cloaks promised at least three people. Maybe more. But their ineptness eased him; skilled assassins didn't clomp their way through forest or get so close. This was personal.

Moments later, four men burst forth from the trees, one bellowing, "*A Kerr!*"

A grim smile twisted Lachlan's lips. So, his mannerless friend from the Great Hall had decided to attempt vengeance for his undignified departure. Or ransom the ladies. It would be the last mistake he ever made.

"Bastard knight!" called Lord Kerr as he and three men halted about twenty feet away, each brandishing a sword. "Give us the women, and we shall kill you mercifully. We have a taste for Jezebel and virgin this day."

"Ride on," Lachlan growled.

"You are but one man. You think to defeat four? Foolish bastard!"

In a movement so practiced he could have performed it half-asleep, Lachlan retrieved the dagger strapped to his thigh and hurled it. The second man in the row flopped to the ground, bright-red blood spraying from the neck wound.

"*Three*," he replied, baring his teeth like the Beast he was. These Lowlanders were rock-headed to believe they could defeat him on the soil of his ancestors.

Lord Kerr stared at his fallen friend, his face paling. Then, with a high-pitched cry, he charged forward, sword raised, his two remaining men at his side.

Unsheathing his own sword, Lachlan waited. These fools could stumble over the slippery leaves, the barely dried mud, the unkempt road, and raise a sweat. They had chosen to engage rather than depart. He would not grant them a single boon this day.

Lord Kerr's accomplices hindered rather than helped. It soon became clear they were accustomed to threatening rather than fighting; they swung their expensive swords in wide arcs that left their chests and bellies exposed, and their thrusts were weak and easily turned aside. Almost lazily, he helped them both unto judgment with two brutal slashes that spilled their innards onto the ground.

"Penniless, landless bastard," spat Lord Kerr, now a defiant army of one. "Fed scraps from the noble table like a dog your whole life. I won't kill you quite yet. Just maim. I'll let you watch me fuck your women, over and over. They'll scream and cry, but you'll be able to do naught. Except know how badly you failed."

Lachlan merely stared, his gaze unblinking. The word "bastard" had long ago lost the power to hurt. Besides, the man would not get near the king's precious jewels, let alone hurt them. "Kill me?" he challenged. "Try, then."

The Lowlander lunged, and their swords clashed, the metallic shriek overloud in the stillness of the roadside. Lord Kerr was far more competent than his men and driven by hurt pride, unflagging in his attack. But Lachlan had the superior height, reach, and strength advantage, and the older man soon dripped blood from several deep cuts.

"Son of a whore!" said his enemy, feinting left, then right, stabbing at Lachlan's left shoulder. The sword tip parted the fabric of his shirt and doublet and took some flesh with it, a stinging reminder of his mortality.

His temper reignited, Lachlan's sword arced and slashed through the air in a deadly dance and at last forced the Lowlander to his knees. "Yield."

"Never."

"*Yield.*"

Lord Kerr laughed. "I'll return, you know. You'll not be free of me. I'll bring the best warriors in Scotland, and we'll butcher you slowly. Tar and feather—no, crushed on the wheel like the baseborn sinner you are. I should like to watch that. I'll make your women watch too. The king will get them back for gold, but they'll be broken. So very broken. And they'll deserve it, the whore and the traitor's daughter…"

The word hung in the air like heavy mist, and the Lowlander looked at him in confusion. Then his body fell one way, his head the other.

Lachlan sucked in slow, deep breaths to ease his racing heart. Today his victory was a rather hollow one; while he had killed countless on the battlefield and resolved many a "delicate matter" for the king, this was a little different. He had slain a Scottish nobleman. There would be much to explain and seek penance for.

"Driver!" he called, and the man ran over. "Wrap and bury them. With a cross. And a prayer…for their souls."

"Aye, sir!"

His cut shoulder burning, Lachlan did his best to wipe away the other men's blood spray with his shirtsleeve as he marched back to the wagon. He could only imagine how feral he looked, but he needed to see with his own eyes that the ladies were unharmed.

"Lady Janet. Lady Marjorie. All is well."

Moments later, the leather rolled up, and two faces peered out the back of the wagon. He breathed a sigh of relief. Shaken, but unhurt.

"S-Sir Lachlan!" stammered Lady Marjorie, her blue eyes huge. "Are you injured?"

"Nay, lady," he said swiftly. "Not my blood."

"Who were they?" said Lady Janet calmly, a woman who had seen and heard many things as the king's mistress. "Do you know?"

"Lord Kerr. Three others."

Lady Marjorie gasped. "From the Great Hall? Then this is my fault."

"No, dear one," said Lady Janet, smoothing her ward's hair. "They chose to attack. The most foolish men in Scotland, to take on Sir Lachlan."

His cheeks warmed at the brisk praise, but in truth he

would have preferred the hair smooth, filthy as he was. Apart from Lady Marjorie's touch of gratitude in the Great Hall, how long had it been since he'd felt a woman's soothing hands? It was hard to remember. But he well knew how good Lady Janet's hand felt; he had lain awake for hours after leaving her alone outside her chamber. Both he and his cock had been more than a little angry at the king for his interference. Lachlan had probably looked like Lady Marjorie did now, all closed eyes and parted lips, silently pleading for more.

Envy surged through him, alongside a swift resurgence of fierce lust.

Now that the battle was won and his ladies safe, the familiar need rose in him to celebrate victory in his favored way: to rut until spent. Alas, this day he would find companionship with his palm rather than a warm, wet, and eager cunt.

Lachlan cleared his throat. "Loch Leven is nearby. We can camp there. The water is fresh…the fish are p-plentiful. As are the f-fowl."

Damn his affliction! He'd been doing so well, and now Lady Janet's brow furrowed.

"Are you sure you are unhurt?"

"Aye."

"Good," she said softly. "For when we reach the loch, I must speak privately with you. The matter we discussed outside my chamber…must be brought to conclusion."

All the air left him. Surely he couldn't be so fortunate.

Could he?

Lachlan inclined his head. "As you wish, lady."

The mile or so to camp would be the longest of his life.

But if such a reward awaited him…no hardship at all.

Chapter Four

"Thank you for this. Forgive me for being such a poor traveling companion."

Janet smiled reassuringly as she expertly mixed a pinch of powdered herbal sleeping draught with watered wine for Marjorie. She had begun to droop during the simple but delicious evening meal of fresh fish that Sir Lachlan had caught and cooked over the campfire. Now her face was gray with fatigue, and her eyes were shadowed. "Think nothing of it, my dear. Wagon travel is ghastly at the best of times, even more so for someone unused to it. I much prefer horseback myself, but the king did insist…and to be fair, he was correct to think of our safety."

Nodding, Marjorie shifted on the wagon bench to make herself more comfortable. "Sir Lachlan had a lot of blood on him. I'm glad…I'm glad I did not see what happened—what we heard was bad enough. Do you think he told the truth when he said he was unhurt?"

A proper guardian would lie to protect delicate sensibilities. Alas, she would never be a proper guardian, as she had already demonstrated in stroking her ward to a screaming release.

"I'm not sure," Janet admitted. "I do not think badly injured, for he moved all limbs freely in setting up camp and catching the fish. But maybe there are wounds he concealed. I suspect Sir Lachlan is not a man who would readily reveal pain or ask for assistance."

"No," said Marjorie. "Will you tend to him? I don't like thinking he has no one. I would do so, but I can scarcely keep my eyes open."

Janet kept her gaze on the herbal concoction. Indeed, she would shortly be tending to Sir Lachlan most thoroughly. Not just for his benefit but to ease her unfulfilled needs too. After her earlier interlude with Marjorie—and Lachlan saving them both from those vile Lowland vermin before silently, stoically, serving them food on bended knee—her emotions were in turmoil and threatening to burst forth. But she could not allow herself to open her heart to either her ward or her protector. She'd already had Aileen and Fergus snatched from her, and she could not endure such terrible pain again.

No. Pleasure was the only thing required to restore her peace of mind. No hearts, no flowers, and certainly no falling in love. All she wanted was a willing, obedient man underneath her to ride into the blessed oblivion of release.

"Yes," Janet replied softly. "I will tend to him. After I have tended to you."

"You are so good to me."

Before Janet could reply, Marjorie leaned forward and kissed her cheek. A brief, awkward kiss from a blushing virgin who hadn't yet learned the power of her lips and tongue, but she felt it like a brand, a lightning bolt that scorched between her legs and caused her pearl to throb.

This most certainly would not do.

Janet set down the pewter goblet of sleeping draught and

gave her ward a stern frown. "You forget my instruction from earlier this day. Impatience is disobedience. And what is the punishment for disobedience?"

Marjorie quivered. "Pleasure is withheld."

"Indeed. When we get to St. Andrews, a good ward—an obedient ward—could learn all the secrets of love. Pleasure so great, her earlier release would be as a puddle is to a loch. However, a disobedient ward will remain innocent as a little lamb until the king decides her husband," she finished idly, tracing a fingertip across the other woman's lips before trailing it down the side of her neck, along her collarbone, delving under the bodice of her linen shift to stroke the tops of her ample breasts.

Marjorie whimpered, and Janet punished her further by allowing that fingertip free rein to circle the younger woman's distended nipples but not to touch them. Once. Twice. Then she withdrew her hand and reached for the goblet. "Drink. You will feel much refreshed after a good sleep."

Still trembling, Marjorie downed the contents in one swallow. Then she lay down on the bench and pulled up her fur covers. "You will be kind to Sir Lachlan?" she mumbled, her eyes closing. "He needs kindness. He's so lonely. Like me."

Janet froze, but moments later, her ward was fast asleep. Rather a relief, as she'd been on the verge of taking the younger woman into her arms. Holding her close.

Irritable at her own weakness and dressed only in her shift and a fur-lined robe, Janet climbed out of the wagon and stalked toward the campfire. In her hand, she held her leather satchel containing fresh batches of tonics, ointments, and neatly rolled linen bandages, and the small glass bottles and dishes clinked together with her strides. That sound was nothing compared to the driver's ale-induced snores over to the left, but this night she would leave him be. In that he'd witnessed all Sir Lachlan's kills, maybe assisted in the burials, the man deserved all the flagons he'd consumed, and good rest...

Devil take it.

Janet stared in dismay at the sight of Sir Lachlan perched on a fallen log, attempting to dab at a gash at his shoulder with a rag, his grimace visible even in just firelight. A dull resignation, too, as though long used to tending to himself.

He needs kindness. He's so lonely. Like me.

"Stop," she barked as Marjorie's words echoed in her mind.

Sir Lachlan stilled. "Lady?"

Marching up to him, her shift and robe billowing about her legs, Janet halted and dropped her herb satchel to the ground. "Do not dare put that filthy rag near your shoulder. I shall tend your battle wound. The wound you neglected to inform me of."

"'Tis but a scratch," he said gruffly. "You need not scold... as my late mother did."

"Clearly a woman of greater sense than you. I am the healer; I decide what a scratch is and is not. Take off your doublet and shirt."

Sir Lachlan silently complied, and she caught her breath at the revelation of his chest, stomach, and arms. The kind of muscles sculpted by vigorous activity...vigorous deadly activity, for his swarthy, hair-roughened flesh was marred by countless scars. Some stitched. Some cauterized. Long-faded white to pink and healing.

It should have been ugly, enough to turn her stomach. And yet this warrior, this Highland Beast, caused a fierce lust in her that no man had before. Not the king. Not her late husband or any of the other men at court.

Only him.

"You don't have to," he rasped into the silence. "I know

I'm…it's not fit for…a lady."

Janet gritted her teeth against another unwanted surge of emotion. Bad enough she'd been tempted to hold and soothe Marjorie, but now Sir Lachlan also? She needed to take command of the situation, reestablish control, and outline terms for a possible bedding-only affair. Certainly nothing more.

"Hush, now," she said briskly. "And let me explain how matters will proceed. I know you are named Beast, but you'll be docile as a newborn kitten while I attend to your shoulder. It is not a deep cut but needs to be cleaned and bound to prevent infection. Then…you and I shall talk terms."

"Terms?" Sir Lachlan asked hesitantly, but there was a glimmer of something in his dark eyes that looked painfully like hope. Damn him!

"Quite. For an affair."

...

Lady Janet wanted an affair.

Lachlan wrestled with the thought as she rummaged through her satchel, then withdrew two glass bottles and a neat roll of clean linen bandage.

As in the king's chamber when he'd discovered his future, he was in two minds. A part of him rejoiced at the thought of having her in his arms, of obeying her instructions and bringing her pleasure. A part of him was crushed that she wanted no more than that, even as he understood no highborn lady desired to wed a landless bastard whose looks were best described as frightening. Only a fool wished for the stars. But even as his soul yearned for more, his damned body—with its fierce craving to be touched, to be commanded by an experienced woman—made the decision for him.

"Your terms?" he said abruptly.

Lady Janet smiled, as aided by the light of the roaring campfire, her nimble fingers cleaned his shoulder with an herbal concoction that stung his skin. Then she smoothed a thick, cooling peppermint-scented poultice across it and lastly covered it in a bandage that she looped under his arm and fastened with a knot. "After our interrupted discussion at Stirling, I believe you understand my preference to lead and are content with such an arrangement. But I have other rules. I expect loyalty from my lovers for the duration of the affair; I do not appreciate those who stray. I expect a man to use his tongue and his fingers as well as his cock. And I expect him to advise me if at any time he does not like something. Pleasure is pleasure for all, not one. Do you accept?"

"Yes."

"Your terms?" she asked.

Love me, as I love you.

"Time," Lachlan said hoarsely. "I mean, er...time outside bed. Together."

Lady Janet nodded, her eyes growing heavy lidded. "Very well. Shall we begin?"

"Wait. Should I spill...inside or outside?"

She frowned. "It matters not. Surely you know that I am barren."

"What do you wish?"

Lady Janet's frown cleared, and it was like the sun appearing from behind a cloud as she smiled approvingly. "An excellent question. I rather like inside. Nothing to distract from that glorious end. Now, Beast, are you ready to be ridden? For I know I am ready to ride."

His cock surged, a fervent *yes* to the suggestion. But damn it, he needed her taste in his mouth. "You said...tongue and fingers."

"So I did," she purred, discarding her robe and spreading it across the log before sitting upon it and parting her thighs.

"Kneel."

Disobediently, Lachlan turned and brushed his mouth against hers, eager to know the softness of her lips first. She made a sound of surprise, but moments later those nimble fingers cupped his face, angling his head, and her tongue darted against his lips, demanding entry. He surrendered at once, delighting in the firm and hungry expertise of her kiss until she drew away.

"My nipples," she said huskily. "Suck them. Hard."

Lachlan nodded, his heart thumping with excitement as he moved to kneel between her legs, watching closely as Lady Janet tugged down the bodice of her shift. Her breasts were small, dusted with freckles, and tipped with pale-brown nipples. When she cupped one breast and offered it to him, he fell on it like a starving man, taking the entire perfect little mound into his mouth. Sucking. Biting. Licking. Rasping her with his short beard.

"Forgive me—"

"I like it," she gasped. "The other. Suck the other. Now."

He'd have happily attended to her nipples for hours, but soon her hands pressed on his shoulders, an unspoken instruction for him to move lower. Disappointment flashed through him at the gentleness of the action, but of course a lady born couldn't know the true depth of his most secret and depraved need—to be forced, to be *taken* rough and hard by the woman he loved. Yet he couldn't stay disappointed for long, not when such a reward awaited him.

The spicy scent of Lady Janet's cunt teased his nose, her bush flaming red like her hair, and Lachlan reverently parted the crisp curls to reveal the slick pink folds and her swollen pearl. Unable to resist, he dragged his tongue from her entrance up to her pearl. Her flavor exploded in his mouth, addicting him forever, and with a fierce growl, he settled in to feast.

Lady Janet moaned. "Yes, just like that. A bit higher. *Mmmm.* Lick my pearl, a little to the side...oh heavens, yes. There. Now fuck me with your tongue. Deep. *Yes*, Lachlan. Ohhhhh..."

Joy surged through him when her hips jerked, her mound grinding against his face as her inner walls pulsed around his tongue and sweet honey trickled down his throat. Greedy for more, to hear his name again as a keening release, Lachlan lapped at her folds. Then he licked his way up to her pearl, circling it with just the tip of his tongue before fastening his lips around the swollen bud and sucking it until she bucked against him with a wild cry.

About to start again, Lachlan was halted by a sharp tug on his hair so good he almost spilled his seed. He glanced up. "Lady?" he asked, knowing he'd brought her pleasure and yet equally concerned he'd failed her in some way.

"I have need of your cock in my cunt," she said harshly, her eyes glittering in the firelight, her cheeks flushed with passion. "*Now.*"

A little unsteadily, Lachlan rose to his feet and tugged down his hose before sitting on the log atop Lady Janet's robe. His cock bobbed against his stomach, harder than stone, and when she wrapped her fingers around him and squeezed, he gasped in agonized pleasure as his seed dampened her fingers.

Praying he wouldn't disgrace himself like the greenest of lads, he began mumbling in Gaelic.

"It won't help, you know," said Lady Janet with a wicked grin as she tormented his balls and the dripping head of his cock with feather-light strokes. "The counting."

"You know Gaelic?"

"Oh yes. My father thought it too vulgar for a lady, which is precisely why I took it upon myself to find a tutor. I make my own rules, like taking a Beast for my pet."

The words were teasing, but Lachlan shuddered in fierce yearning. To belong to Lady Janet in every way, to serve and cherish and protect her the rest of their days…

Thankfully such whimsy halted when she straddled him, and slowly, so slowly, the hottest, wettest, most exquisite cunt in Scotland swallowed his cock whole. Aye, Lady Janet was a miracle, a marvel, and as she rode him like an expert horsewoman, he could only groan in grateful ecstasy.

When she took his hand and guided it between her legs, he thought she wished him to stroke her pearl, but she shook her head.

"Wet your finger," she commanded between panting breaths. When he complied, she moved his hand to her arse. "Enter me."

"There?" Lachlan replied, stunned that Lady Janet knew of such forbidden pleasures when he should not be. Of course this lusty angel would know. Gently, he penetrated her back entrance with just a fingertip, rocking it back and forth in time with his cock.

"Yes. Oh yes."

Moments later Lady Janet fell forward, muffling her scream of release by biting his shoulder. The tiny jolt of pleasure-pain shoved him over the edge into bliss, a low roar tearing from his throat as his seed flooded the sweet haven of her cunt.

Indeed this night, he had witnessed a glimpse of heaven.

All he would ever see.

• • •

She'd had the deepest sleep of her life. But now her skin was clammy with perspiration under the pile of too-warm furs, and abruptly; that, and the confines of the wagon were suffocating her.

Air. She needed fresh air. And some cold water to splash on her face and arms.

Shoving away the furs, Marjorie sat up on the bench before carefully opening her trunk and retrieving a simple brocade robe to put on over her linen shift. When she got to her feet and began to move toward the rear of the wagon, a floorboard creaked under her, and she glanced back with an apologetic wince. Fortunately, Janet did not stir.

Once she had mastered the ties and hooks fastening the leather cover, Marjorie scrambled out of the wagon with a deep sigh of relief. The morning was cool—a little gray overhead, but the air wonderfully fresh—and away in the distance, the birds that called Loch Leven home were noisily announcing the arrival of a new day.

Freedom.

The word twirled around in her mind. At this moment, with no audience, no rules, she could do whatever she pleased…a thought both heady and terrifying. What did people do when their life was not governed each moment by bells and orders, straps and prayer?

Wet your feet in the loch. The prioress would never have permitted such a thing.

Before she could change her mind, Marjorie hurried past their snoring driver, the smoldering campfire, and the canvas tent where Sir Lachlan slept, down to the water's edge.

Then stopped. And gulped.

This close, Loch Leven was nothing short of daunting. The blue-green expanse stretched for miles and miles, more than enough to drown her and swallow her body forever. Considering she'd never stood in water more than ankle deep—those rare times the prioress had permitted usage of the copper tub for bathing—and could not swim, even being near the loch was dangerous and rather foolish. But if she did not at least try to face this fear, how would she ever overcome it?

Courage, Marjorie.

Straightening her shoulders, Marjorie leaned down and gathered up the hems of her shift and robe, twisting them into a large, loose knot. Now her legs were scandalously bared to the knee, but it would be easier to wade with the fabric out of the way. One deep, shuddering breath, and she inched forward until the cold loch waters lapped at her toes.

By the saints, this was difficult.

"Too cold, lady?"

She yelped, almost losing her footing, and only a huge paw under her elbow halted an unceremonious face-first bath. "Sir Lachlan. Once again, I did not hear you. I think I need to affix a bell around your neck."

One thick black brow lifted. "Should I cough?"

"Yes. Or hire a troubadour. *Sir Lachlan approaches!* At least until I no longer jump a foot in the air."

"I frighten you."

Marjorie hesitated at the flat words that somehow held a great deal of feeling. "No," she said softly. "You have been naught but kind to me. But you are the size of a mountain, and you move so quietly, with such grace. And I am so unused to men…"

"I'll make a sound," he said, nodding. "Will you swim?"

"I cannot swim. Actually, this is my first time in a loch. I thought to wade just a little, but I am not as brave as I thought."

"You are brave," Sir Lachlan said, frowning. Then he held out his hand. "Come. We'll wade together."

Her heart leaped, and Marjorie bit her lip. Although he neither kissed hands nor read poetry, this knight captivated her far more than was fair. An ice-blooded warrior of few words, and yet the way he watched over her and Janet felt like more than duty. If only she wasn't the king's ward and obligated to marry where *he* wished. "You are the best of men," she said. "But your hose and stockings—"

"They will dry. Come."

Gripping his hand, Marjorie gingerly followed him into the water. Ankle deep. Calf. *Knee.* It was unnerving, and the water chilled her skin as little waves sloshed against her legs, yet it was so refreshing she sighed. "Oh, that's lovely."

"Freshwater loch. Good for bathing. And cleaning linen."

"Oh, certainly. I—"

Marjorie lost her words entirely as something nudged her leg. Something *slimy*. A shriek tore from her throat, and she threw herself at Sir Lachlan, wrapping her arms and legs around him and clinging like a kitten to a tapestry. Somehow he didn't stumble under her weight or drop her in the water. In fact, with nary a blink, he merely curved one bulging arm under her bottom as a sort of seat.

His lips twitched. "You're safe, lady."

"What was that?" she spluttered.

"A fish?"

Marjorie groaned inwardly. A shriek to wake the dead and a leap as though pursued by rabid wolves…for a *fish*. "Does it not know we supped on them last evening? We are *death* to fish! It should be rushing to warn its friends and family, not…not…kissing my leg!"

Sir Lachlan shuddered, and an odd choking sound emerged. "Indeed. Not sporting."

"Are you *laughing* at me, sir? When I was just accosted by a monster of the sea?"

"Of the loch," he replied, his shoulders now shaking. "And no. Never."

Amusement transformed his face. His brown eyes gleamed, attractive little lines appeared at either side of his mouth, and just for a moment that air of lonely heaviness that usually surrounded him rose.

She had done that. Made the Highland Beast smile.

"Fortunate for you," she said pertly, knowing she was too heavy a burden yet selfishly unwilling to let his warm, hard body go. Not when the risk of more fish kisses remained. "Everyone thinks I am a kitten. But I am a fierce full-grown cat. With claws."

"Yes," he rasped.

At the odd change in his tone, Marjorie glanced down.

Oh *no*.

Her robe had slipped right off her shoulder, fully exposing the rounded neckline of her linen shift…and the tops of her breasts. Worse, in the cool air, her nipples were visible hard points, straining against the fabric.

Mortified, Marjorie tried to shrug the robe back up. As she wriggled against Sir Lachlan, trying desperately to cover herself, she only succeeded in rubbing her breasts against his chest.

Oh. It felt *good*.

She had always been starved of the touch she craved. Yesterday, Janet had unleashed something inside her, a need she could no longer deny, and now she couldn't halt her wayward body from seeking more. With a helpless whimper, she deliberately rubbed her aching, tingling nipples against his chest.

Sir Lachlan sucked in a harsh breath. "Lady—"

"What on earth are you two doing?"

Marjorie froze. Over his shoulder, about twenty feet away, Janet stood on the shoreline, fully dressed in her red velvet traveling gown, her arms folded. Sir Lachlan went rigid, and Marjorie quickly slid down his body back into the water, then stepped well away from him.

"Good morning," said Marjorie awkwardly to her guardian, her cheeks burning. How could she even explain such unseemly behavior? "There was a, er…fish."

Janet tilted her head. "In a loch, I'd wager many," she replied coolly. "But you should get dressed so we might break bread and then recommence our journey. The driver is readying the horses."

"Of course."

Miserable, unable to meet Sir Lachlan's eyes after her shameful display, Marjorie waded back to shore. Janet had been so kind, so generous, had deigned to show her the most exquisite pleasure imaginable, and this was how she repaid her.

Why could she never do anything right?

Chapter Five

The rest of the journey to St. Andrews passed without incident; rather unfortunate, when he wanted nothing more than to take out his frustration on some hapless brigand.

Lachlan slowed Storm to his least-favored pace, a slow walk, as they approached the stone wall announcing the boundary of the king's former property, the estate now belonging to Lady Janet.

How could he have been such a damned fool?

She had told him she required loyalty from a lover. That she did not appreciate straying. And the very next day, he'd had another woman in his arms: her virgin ward.

A woman he'd been overwhelmingly tempted by.

Lady Marjorie was sweet. So innocent. She'd made him laugh with her jests about the fish. But there had been nothing sweet or innocent in the way she'd rubbed her ample breasts against him and scraped his chest with large pink nipples that her shift hadn't fully concealed. Or the needy little whimper. Lady Marjorie might have been imprisoned in a convent most of her life, but like water rising behind a wall of sand, he suspected she was ready to burst forth and embrace the ways of lust. That made her a threat to both his willpower and peace of mind. To bed her, even to want her, would be to betray Lady Janet and his friend the king.

Unthinkable.

"This the place, sir?" the wagon driver asked, breaking into his thoughts.

Lachlan glanced back at him, and the man gave him a look of such naked hope that he almost smiled. The driver would return home to Stirling in the morning, and it seemed that after their eventful journey, that moment could not come swiftly enough. "Aye," Lachlan said.

"Very nice. All them trees to lessen the ocean winds, a little stream...fine home too. The ladies will be happy here."

That remained to be seen. St. Andrews had gathered many great minds, and Scotland's first university had been founded by papal bull nearly one hundred years prior. Lady Janet would probably enjoy renewing acquaintances she'd made through the king and her late husband, and challenging the scholars with her learning and bold opinions. But the small town was also an ecclesiastical center, with pilgrims from all corners journeying to the ancient cathedral. In that she had never seen eye to eye with the church, and Lady Marjorie had endured such an unpleasant experience in her convent—not to mention that Lady Janet had always shone in the glittering, unruly world of the Scottish court...

Lachlan grimaced. Paradise or purgatory.

With a light click of Storm's reins, they moved toward the sturdy wooden gate. Moments later, an armed guard appeared.

"Halt in the name of—oh, good evening, Sir Lachlan. The ladies are in the wagon?"

"Aye," he replied, grunting in approval at the alert guard, the gate that swung open on well-oiled hinges, and the wall in good repair. James might have visited the place only a few times each year, but they were prepared. "Ready for supper. And rest."

The guard nodded. "All is well. The king sent word, and the servants are eager to welcome their new mistress."

"Good," said Lachlan, riding on. The path from the gate to the manor was well kept and free of rocks; no doubt the ladies would appreciate it. He couldn't imagine how sore they would be after two days' travel in a wagon. A few years prior, during a bloody battle with a few clan chiefs who'd rebelled against the king's authority, he had been injured and transported in such a manner. *Torturous* was the word he would use to describe that swaying, jolting journey.

As soon as he dismounted, a young lad bounded up to take Storm away to the stables to be fed and watered, giving him time for a brief inspection of the manor while he waited for the wagon.

Folding his arms, Lachlan let his gaze travel over the large modern stone buildings. Indeed, they were fit for a king. To the left sat the kitchens, buttery, larder, and granary, connected to the main manor by a covered walkway. The ground floor included the hall, warmed by two fireplaces, and a chapel. Upstairs were the private rooms—the bedchambers and a solar for the ladies to read, play music, or embroider in. Over to the right were the flower and herb gardens, an orchard, and he could hear the faint sound of the stream splashing against small rocks as it wound its way toward the sea. Further afield were the king's hunting grounds, an expanse of deep-green forest that he would make full use of to provide fowl and meat for the table.

"Lachlan! Help me down from this devil-plagued contraption."

He stifled a grin. The wagon hadn't even stopped moving, and Lady Janet near dangled from the back in her haste to be free of the confinement. "Aye, lady."

He marched over to carefully tug free the rest of the leather cover that she had partially opened. Then he reached up, gripped Lady Janet's waist, and lowered her to the ground. Just for a moment, she slumped against him, and he grimaced in sympathy as he took the opportunity to touch her further, rubbing her back as gently as he could.

"I swear, by all the saints, I am never traveling in a wagon again," she muttered, actually permitting him to ease her aching body, and his heart leaped.

"No need," he replied. "Fine stable here."

Far sooner than he wished, Lady Janet stepped away and smiled wearily. "I'm glad to hear it, although all I want this night is something that does not move, so soft I can sink into it. Oh yes, and enough wine to launch a ship."

"You'll have it," he promised, glancing over to see dozens of servants gathering on the steps of the manor to welcome them. "All is ready."

"I shall go and greet the servants. Would you assist Marjorie for me? She is not well."

Lachlan hesitated, but it was concern in her gaze rather than anger or trickery, and he nodded. "We'll meet you…in the hall."

When he turned back to the wagon, Lady Marjorie was waiting for him, face pale and shoulders stooped with fatigue. Wordlessly, he reached up for her, and she near flopped into his arms. At first he set her on the ground, but when her legs buckled, he scooped her up, and she looked at him, her eyes glistening with tears.

"I do not like wagon travel," she whispered, burying her face in his shoulder.

"Worse than fish kisses," he replied gruffly, hating to see her upset, but when Lady Marjorie's laugh was watery at best, he added quickly, "Don't cry. There'll be wine."

"Wine is well and good, but all I want is bed."

Lachlan gritted his teeth. Only the worst of men would think lustful thoughts of a highborn virgin in desperate need of rest and comfort. Yet his mind taunted him with a vision of Lady Marjorie in the thin shift that concealed nothing, reclining on a large pile of pillows, reaching for him…demanding he pleasure her with his mouth…demanding he take her…

No.

He needed to stay as far away as possible until this madness passed. He loved and wanted Lady Janet. Had done so for years, and those feelings had not dimmed one bit. A good man—a worthy man—did not have tender feelings for more than one woman.

Indeed, if he just avoided Lady Marjorie, all would be well.

Surely.

...

When Sir Lachlan carried her from the wagon into the manor so easily, so carefully, she had wanted to cling to his broad chest and never let go. Now, when the three of them sat at the end of the long rectangular oak table, eating supper, he wouldn't meet her gaze.

And it was entirely her fault. He wasn't her husband, betrothed, or family member but a bodyguard appointed by the king. Yet she kept touching him, throwing herself at him, when he clearly did not wish her to do so. Just because she admired him did not mean he returned the sentiment, and she needed to accept that like a sensible grown woman.

Alas, far easier said than done.

Unhappily, Marjorie mopped up the last of her delicious chicken-and-vegetable broth with a chunk of soft white bread. As though the cook and kitchen staff knew exactly how tired they all were, how unsettled their stomachs and aching their bones, they had served a simple, tasty supper that didn't require any carving—and, as promised, a great deal of French wine. But even as her body sighed with appreciation, her spirits remained low, and for a moment she missed the familiarity of the convent. She had disliked the strictness and confinement, but at least she'd known her place in the world. Outside it, she walked on a cliff edge, always unsure if the next thing she said or did would be acceptable or deserving of reprimand or punishment. The rules were just so...arbitrary. A woman could be celebrated or shunned for a deed at any given moment, and on many occasions, both.

She turned to Janet, who sat at the head of the table. "How do you find your broth?"

"I never thought chicken broth would be worthy of song, but I'm tempted. Much as I love a feast, I have no desire to fall asleep atop a boar's head or dressed goose. The kitchen staff—actually, all the servants here are excellent. I was cautious, understanding full well that they would know of me and might disapprove of the choices I've made in my life. But none have as much as quirked an eyebrow."

Sir Lachlan took a gulp of wine, then cleared his throat. "If anyone should...tell me. I will resolve it."

Janet grinned and leaned over to pat his hand. "You are a treasure. But I am quite adept at thunder and brimstone when the need arises. Everyone soon learns that life is pleasant when my rules are obeyed."

"Very pleasant," he rasped, and Janet's cheeks went a little pink.

Marjorie stilled at the banked heat, the knowledge and intimacy in their exchanged glance.

Of course. Janet and Sir Lachlan were lovers.

Embarrassment at how long it had taken for her to see the

plainly obvious made her wince, but another emotion swiftly engulfed that: pure envy. Janet, a widow, and Sir Lachlan, a bachelor, had all the freedom in the world to indulge in an affair. Especially now that Janet had her own land, her own home. It was all so unfair. Because of her late father's actions, Marjorie had been imprisoned for sixteen years, and now, rather than being able to choose a younger, virile lover like Sir Lachlan, she would be forced to wed at the king's desire. Yes, Janet had said the king was a romantic at heart and not to give up hope of a happy marriage, but it was hard to imagine that outcome. She'd seen the men at court, the nobles and lairds and dignitaries. Marriages were never a reward for the lady but usually for a man's long service to the crown or to join the lands of two great families.

A scream of frustration about to tear from deep inside her, Marjorie abruptly pushed back her chair and got to her feet. "Forgive me, Janet, Sir Lachlan. My, ah, stomach is still unsettled after the journey, and I would like nothing more than to lie down."

Sir Lachlan stared at her, his lips parting as though he might speak before they clamped shut.

Janet's gaze was all sympathy. "Poor dear. I had the servants put your trunks upstairs in the chamber next to mine. Second door on the left side of the hallway. I'll send up some hot water for a sponge bath and visit you later."

"Thank you. Good evening," said Marjorie with a curtsy, then she turned and walked out of the dining hall.

Fortunately it was not yet dark outside, and with the manor boasting a number of windows with expensive glass panes, she could see without the need for a torch or candle. The stairs were wooden, and while she winced a little at the heavy thud of her footsteps, at least they weren't spiral to make her head spin more than it already was.

When she opened the door to her chamber, her breath

caught.

Oh. It was lovely.

Not especially large but generously furnished. Intricate tapestries of unicorns at play and maidens picking flowers hung from the walls to stop draughts, and the woven rugs on the floor were thick enough for her shoes to sink into. Two windows with shutters to keep out the wind and rain overlooked the gardens, and a fire had already been lit in the small stone hearth. A cushioned chair and table sat in front of the fire, but her gaze stopped worshipfully on the four-poster bed on the other side of the room. Not a cot or a pallet or a wooden board, but a *bed*.

Marjorie moaned as she hurried to it, yanking the embroidered quilts back to reveal crisp linen sheets covering a feather mattress with no sag. It looked *new*. About ready to hurl herself onto it and sleep for a hundred years, she halted when a knock at the open door revealed a smiling servant with a bowl of steaming water and a cloth.

"For you, milady. The mistress ordered it. I'll just put it over here on the stand."

"Thank you."

"No trouble. You need anything, just ask. We're glad to have you here. Serving the king was a great honor, but he only visited a few times each year. Steady employment is a boon."

Marjorie nodded. "This room is beautiful."

"Aye. The king oversaw all the furnishings, you know. He's a man of refined tastes. Loves them French fashions, even if he didn't always love the French. This James is a good one, unlike him before."

Stifling a laugh at the older woman's plain speaking, so typical of a Highlander, Marjorie nodded again. "May the king prosper."

"Do you need help with your gown?"

"Please."

Once the servant departed, Marjorie went to the bowl of hot water, dipped the cloth in, and wiped it over her face and body. Oh, it felt nice. Then she went to her trunk and found a fresh linen nightgown and her most prized possession: a silver comb that had belonged to her mother. Attending to her long tresses was a necessary chore; if she did not, they would be a bird's nest by morning.

Grimacing, she began to tug the comb through her hair. "Ow!"

"Easy, my dear," said a familiar female voice laced with amusement. "Few ladies have the bone structure to suit baldness. Let me comb it for you."

Marjorie glanced over at Janet. Her lips were plump and pink—clearly she'd been recently and quite thoroughly kissed—and that stab of envy surged through her again. "Sir Lachlan has retired?"

"No, he's gone to inspect the manor and grounds. He takes his duties very seriously, fortunately for us. We have plenty of time to discuss your attraction to him."

Her comb clattered onto the stone floor.

• • •

Her ward's expression was part stricken, part guilt, part rabbit caught in torchlight, and on another occasion Janet might have laughed. Courtiers well knew her habit of saying what needed to be said rather than dancing around the topic, but of course Marjorie didn't. No doubt she was accustomed to diversion and dissembling, if she got conversation at all.

But they did need to talk about this, and a few of her unbreakable guardian rules.

Leaning down, Janet retrieved the pretty silver comb from the floor. "Marjorie—"

"Forgive me," Marjorie blurted, twisting her hands

together. "I feel so foolish that I didn't see. I will stay right away from him. Please don't be angry for what I did at the loch."

"What did you do? Tell the truth, now," she replied sternly. Her ward needed to learn that openness was critical between them. Many things would be tolerated under this roof, but trickery and falsehoods were not in that number.

Marjorie stared at the floor, her cheeks crimson. "I...I... rubbed my breasts against his chest."

"I see. Did Sir Lachlan wish you to do that?"

"I don't know. He did not say."

Janet tapped the comb against her palm. "Then let that be a second lesson for you. Pleasure must always be pleasure for all, not one. Good men and women ensure their potential lover is willing and excited to be touched. They do not force themselves on another, not even a kiss."

"But how do you know for sure if they are willing?"

"You talk. You tease. They might make a vague suggestion to test the water, so to speak. Or you might. Always beforehand, my dear. If they are receptive, your discussion can become more risqué or even downright wicked. I find erotic talk at the beginning of or during an interlude to be quite, quite seductive, although in fairness not all enjoy it."

Marjorie nodded slowly. "I understand. Like we talked in the wagon, before you showed me how to touch myself. I had a *choice*."

"Exactly. Learn what your lover enjoys and encourage them in turn to learn the same about you. Now, come and sit on the bed, and I'll comb your hair."

Soon they were perched side by side on the feather mattress, and Janet began to slide the comb through Marjorie's thick and unruly brown locks, which fell to the small of her back. It lacked a little shine and was in need of a thorough egg-yolk cleansing followed by a good dousing with rosewater.

"Are you displeased with me?" said Marjorie tentatively. "For being attracted to Sir Lachlan, I mean."

Janet sighed as she attended to a small knot. "No. Attraction is not something you can control. It just happens. You see a man, or a woman, and think they are delicious. There is much to admire about Lachlan. He has worked hard to rise above his birth, has been a loyal friend and companion to the king, and is quite simply the finest swordsman in the realm. Then of course those strong arms and broad chest. What you can control, though, is what you do next."

"I understand."

"Let me make one thing very clear, though, my dear. This is an *unbreakable* rule. You are the king's ward. This means that your first bedding must be with your husband. I wish for you to learn what you will. To have wondrous experiences with lips and tongues and fingers. But to do more than that is to invite the king's anger, and for all his charm and chivalry, James is not a man to be crossed. It would not just be you punished but myself and Lachlan as well. And I cannot allow that."

Marjorie winced, her expression settling into one of resignation. "I know. And I would not hurt either of you for the world."

Janet's heart clenched at the sadness, the frustration, the younger woman felt. It *was* desperately unfair, all the miseries Marjorie had endured through no fault of her own, and now to live a half life, waiting to see whom the king might select as a husband. Yes, James had arranged some excellent matches in the past, such as her own marriage to Fergus, but that did not mean he would choose so well again. Marjorie's husband might not even be a Scots nobleman. If the king wished to strengthen the alliance with England or extend the hand of friendship to France, Spain, or the Low Countries with the offer of a beautiful virgin of noble blood, she could be sent far away to wed a stranger.

Janet paused in her combing as the thought of Marjorie gone twisted something inside her chest.

No.

She would do her best for her temporary ward. Allow her as much freedom as possible to learn her own mind, her own desires and preferences. Definitely not more than that.

Definitely not love.

"Time for bed," she said briskly.

"Yes, Mother," replied Marjorie with an impish little grin as she scrambled to get under the quilts, managing to show a great deal of plump, dimpled thigh and even a glimpse of that thick brown bush in the process.

"*Mother?*" said Janet, appalled even as arousal stirred at the tempting sight. "No thank you. I much prefer Worst Sinner in Scotland. Or Mistress, for brevity."

"Very well. Good night…*Mistress.*"

Oh, but her ward had a streak of pert. When Marjorie grew in confidence and learned to wear clothing that flattered those lush curves rather than gowns better suited for cleaning rags, when she began to own the sensuality lurking in those big blue eyes and pink lips…men would be lining up from here to the continent, eager to be led about by the codpiece. They would let her run amok, never understanding what she truly wanted and needed: to submit to a stern authority, made to ask—nay, *beg* for pleasure—and have it be granted so thoroughly she screamed in ecstasy.

But Janet Fraser knew.

Sliding from the edge of the bed, she walked the few steps to the head, where Marjorie lay propped up against a small mound of pillows. "Good night, my dear. If you are well enough on the morrow, we might…further your education."

Marjorie sucked in a ragged breath, her eyes widening.

"Another lesson? Show me what I might be taught, please."

"Hmm." Janet stroked her own cheek, as though deep in thought. Then she leaned down and used one fingertip to trace the younger woman's lips, circling them again and again until her ward moaned softly. "You need to learn what your mouth and tongue are capable of. Kissing. Sucking. Licking. Do you agree?"

"Yes," she said fervently.

"Excellent. Then we shall meet in the solar at noon… Marjorie, you are quivering. Is your sweet little cunt throbbing?"

Her ward blushed scarlet, but eventually she nodded.

Janet stifled a grin. Marjorie was so delightfully responsive. "Then you may touch yourself. Stroke your pearl until you gain release, just like I showed you in the wagon. It will help relax you, and you'll sleep better. Until tomorrow, then."

Marjorie nodded, her hand already moving under the quilts. Satisfied she was back in control, Janet turned and walked toward the door.

Hopefully Lachlan had finished his inspections.

She required him for another duty entirely.

Chapter Six

Plague take it, imagining herself as a Thoroughbred, sleek and swift, had not worked. Her pursuers nearly had her cornered.

Marjorie clung to the stair banister, her knees wobbling and breasts aching after the short run.

"I shall fight to the death!" she wheezed, wishing she had a sword to brandish rather than a single waving finger. It did lessen the theatric impact somewhat.

"Lady?"

Marjorie's hand slipped, and she flopped onto the bottom stair in an ungainly heap before turning and glaring at Sir Lachlan. "We agreed on a cough to warn of your approach."

He cleared his throat. "You spoke to no one. Are you well?"

"I did no such thing. I warned away the women stalking me with the food they wish to put in my hair."

Sir Lachlan's brow furrowed. "*Food?*"

Marjorie sighed as her heartbeat finally began to slow. "They claim Janet wishes them to wash my hair. But they don't have a square of lye soap, just a dish of bacon fat. Raw eggs. Vinegar. Now tell me, Sir Lachlan, does that sound like tools of beauty or the makings of supper?"

His head tilted, his gaze suddenly far away. "My mother used eggs. One each month. The chicken had…a bad temper. My hands were pecked bloody. But her hair shone. Like sunbeams."

The silence stretched between them as Marjorie absorbed that halting, rasping affectionate tale, surely the longest string of words Sir Lachlan had ever bestowed upon her. But the emotion behind it—he'd *loved* his mother. It seemed the habit he'd learned as a boy had stayed with the man. He sacrificed and served.

"Is she…is your mother in the Highlands somewhere?"

Sir Lachlan's face shuttered. "No. She died long ago."

"Forgive me, I—"

"Let them wash it," he said gruffly. "To please Lady Janet. It will look…pretty."

And with that pronouncement, he marched past her and out the front door toward the orchard.

Well.

Marjorie propped her chin on her hands and stared after Sir Lachlan. Her head had accepted that he belonged to Janet, that they were lovers, that she had no choice but to remain a virgin until her wedding night with a husband of the king's choosing.

Her heart had yet to reconcile with those facts.

It still believed that Sir Lachlan liked her a little. More than duty, which made it difficult to live under the same roof, as she kept pondering what he and Janet might do together in bed.

Would they ever permit me to watch them?

The shocking thought lodged in her mind, so wicked, so troubling, Marjorie leaped up and paced the entrance hall.

It was sinful enough she wanted so much more from Janet, more touching, to be kissed and stroked and to learn how to do so in return. But to even entertain the thought of watching Janet and Sir Lachlan naked and pleasuring each other, bedding each other...

Marjorie shuddered, her breathing now shallow pants.

Wicked. Terribly, shamefully, wicked. Janet was her guardian, kindly teaching her. Sir Lachlan a protector.

Nothing more.

"Lady Marjorie," came a voice to her left, and she turned to see the two servant women intent on turning her hair into a larder. The curtsies were polite, the expressions exasperated.

She sighed and surrendered. "Very well. Forgive my reluctance, but I've only ever washed my hair with lye soap. I did not know there were other remedies."

One of the women grimaced. "Lye soap? Oh no, m'lady. This will be so much better. No tangles, and it will smell sweet and fresh too."

"Will it take very long? I must meet Lady Janet in the solar at noon. For a, er, lesson."

That I wouldn't miss for the world.

"A half hour at most. We've done it for all the ladies. And our sisters. We'll have your hair looking right nice in no time."

Marjorie shot a doubtful look at the basket. The egg she would try, if for no other reason than Sir Lachlan's poignant story. But bacon fat? Ugh. "Where?"

The other woman smiled. "We have a little bathing tent set up outside for privacy. Hood, gown, and kirtle off; shift on. Come with us and we'll begin."

Soon she knelt on a cushion in front of a large wooden bucket. Several other smaller buckets sat nearby, each filled to the brim with fresh water.

After wetting her hair, two egg yolks were rubbed in.

Then the women rinsed it clean with jugs of water. Next came the bacon fat, and Marjorie's nose twitched at both the smell and the unpleasant cool greasiness on her scalp. Once they'd scraped and rinsed that away, a small deluge of vinegar covered her entire head, trickling onto her arms and down her face, as expert hands firmly massaged. If this was the final treatment, no one would want to sit near her for at least a week. But the vinegar washed away into the wooden bucket, and the servant opened another jar of something green that actually smelled lovely, like fresh herbs.

Marjorie sniffed appreciatively. "Is that mint?"

"Aye, m'lady. Will make your head tingle. Plus parsley, thyme, and watercress made into a paste."

They let the paste sit in her hair for a few minutes before rinsing, then a servant dried away the excess water with a linen towel. Marjorie prepared to stand, but the other servant's voice halted her.

"Two more things, m'lady. We'll rub your hair with silk, then comb it."

She nodded reluctantly, as they were clearly skilled in their work. But when the woman eventually produced a wooden comb, Marjorie gritted her teeth. This was always the worst part.

The comb slid through her hair like an eating knife through tender meat.

"It's not tangled!" she exclaimed. "And it doesn't hurt! It always hurts. Always."

"That's the bacon fat," said the woman with a smug smile. "Egg for shine, vinegar to clean and get rid of any nasties, herbal paste for scent. Rubbing with silk adds extra glow. Aye, your hair is clean as a mountain stream now. But leave your hood off until it has dried fully."

Marjorie sat back on her heels. "I don't know how to thank you."

"The coin we earn is thanks enough. As is a kind mistress. You'll tell Lady Janet you are pleased?"

"Oh yes," she replied, nodding fervently. "When I see her in the solar."

The two women helped her back into her kirtle and cream-colored gown before curtsying and gathering up their buckets and dishes. "Best go on, then, m'lady. Must be nearing noon."

Her heart pounded with anticipation. Janet would be pleased at her obedience, and she could show off her newly beautiful hair. Best of all, it was time for her kissing lesson.

Hurrying to the solar as fast as she could, Marjorie halted in the doorway of the elegantly furnished space, overheated and panting a little. But her gaze raced over the tapestries, the embroidery frame, the harp and lute, and the low table with jugs of wine and sweetmeats atop it, for Janet sat cool and poised on a cushioned chaise in the center of the room.

"Am I late? Forgive me!"

Janet shook her head. "Not at all. I arrived early to inspect the room. We shall enjoy many happy hours here, I'm sure. Come in, my dear. Close the door behind you."

Marjorie's breath hitched as she obeyed the command. "I was getting my hair washed," she said shyly, completing a turn that made her hair whip about her.

"Come and sit next to me so I might see better."

"I rebelled at first," she admitted, perching on the chaise. "The food, you see. I didn't know about eggs and vinegar. Or bacon fat. I was only ever permitted lye soap at the convent. The women here were so kind. So skilled."

"Rebellion?" said Janet, as she leaned forward and wound a lock of washed hair around one finger before tugging it gently. "How wicked."

Marjorie shuddered at the light prickle on her scalp. How could that make other parts of her body feel warm and restless? But there was far more to come, as her guardian traced the outline of her closed lips. Softly at first, then more firmly, until they parted of their own accord. "Mmmmm."

"You sound like a lass ready to learn. Are you?"

She nodded fervently, her breasts bobbing. "Show me. Please."

Janet cradled her cheek, then leaned forward and brushed her lips against Marjorie's. A gentle and delicate kiss, a slow glide of lip against lip.

So soft and sweet!

Yet not nearly enough.

With a frustrated whimper, Marjorie attempted to kiss her back. To her relief and delight, Janet firmed her lips and pressed harder. Soon she felt the flick of Janet's tongue, once, twice. Demanding entry? Uncertain, she tentatively opened her mouth, and her reward was a much deeper and more intimate kiss with a pointed tongue that rubbed against her own, a kiss that sent jolts of hot sensation darting through her body and left her squirming on the chaise.

Overwhelmed, unable to catch her breath, she pulled away.

"Marjorie?" said Janet, he gaze concerned.

"I…I can't breathe," she whispered. "My gown bodice is too tight. May I…may I take it off?"

Her guardian nodded, her eyes glittering like emeralds. "Of course."

• • •

Marjorie was so beautiful. So innocently sensual.

It was taking every bit of willpower she possessed to move slowly in the continuation of this virgin's awakening, for a first kiss was equally important as a first release. Some might say she should have started her lessons with a kiss, but it was her firm opinion that a woman needed to know her own body, her own mind, before sharing it with another.

Pressing her thighs together against a fierce wave of arousal, Janet distracted herself by helping her ward remove her gown and kirtle so she wore only her stockings and shift. The linen garment might be modest, but it barely constrained Marjorie's ample breasts, and her nipples jutted lewdly against the fabric, an unspoken plea to be sucked and bitten and stroked.

This time when Janet leaned in to kiss her, with merciless self-restraint she allowed her own breasts to briefly brush the younger woman's, a tease of soft flesh and hard nipples that promised the world and yet delivered nothing more.

Marjorie moaned.

Stifling her raging lust, Janet feigned confusion. "Something the matter, dear one?"

"I…ah…"

"Tell me," she said sternly.

"My nipples ache terribly. I want to touch them," Marjorie mumbled.

"Touch them how? Stroke? Circle? Pinch?"

Her ward bit her kiss-swollen lip. "I've only stroked them. Never pinched."

Janet nodded. "Depends entirely on the person. Some dislike having their nipples touched at all. Some prefer a light stroking. But others enjoy a hint of pain to heighten sensation and find a pinch very pleasurable."

"Show me?"

"One moment, my dear," said Janet as she sat back on the chaise. She was so unbearably aroused, a moment was needed to clear her head and regain control.

Taking a deep breath, she allowed the tranquility of the solar to drape around her like the softest quilt. It was already her favorite room in the manor, created solely for relaxation and privacy from the noise, the bustle, the *purpose* of the rooms on the ground floor. Today the solar would host a lesson in seduction, but the warmth of the sun shining through the large windows could never compete with the heat between her and Marjorie.

With Sir Lachlan, her lust had been fierce and absolute, a man and a woman who could indulge themselves and had done so because they were a bachelor and a widow with no real restrictions placed upon them. But once had not been enough, nor twice, and in truth she could not see herself willingly giving up her gruff, deadly, and yet delightfully yielding Highland Beast anytime soon. Nor could she deny Marjorie the lessons she so wanted and needed.

By the saints, this was complicated. And the longer she walked this cliff edge, the higher the risk to her heart as it softened toward them both. Her mind already warned her to defy the king and send Sir Lachlan and Marjorie away, but she was on thin ice with James. He had sent a very curt letter expressing his displeasure at the slaying of Lord Kerr and his men; even with the arrows and the threats, the last thing he wanted was a rise in tension between Lowland and Highland. Besides, even the thought of Sir Lachlan and Marjorie gone—knowing that future husbands and wives might never understand their true natures and needs, leaving them lonely and unfulfilled—made her decidedly irritable. Hot tempered in a way only a red-haired Highland lass could be.

"Janet? Are you angry with me?"

At Marjorie's small-voiced question, the dismay on her face, Janet silently berated herself for causing the younger woman anxiety. Where was her command? Her famed skill and experience in lusty matters? She'd admonished her ward last night for not talking before acting, and here she was making the same mistake.

"Not at all, my dear," she replied swiftly, cupping her

cheek and tucking a stray lock of hair behind her ear before trailing her fingers down to the tops of Marjorie's breasts. "Forgive my lapse. I lost my head a little, which is not at all the thing when giving a lesson. Shall we continue?"

Marjorie shuddered, arching her back a little. "*Please.* Touch me."

Deftly, Janet tugged down the bodice of her ward's shift to reveal one creamy, rose pink–tipped breast. Her mouth watered to suck the swollen nipple, to scrape it with her teeth, to bite it. But again she tormented herself with restraint, merely circling the tight bud with her fingertip before sliding one finger on either side and gently squeezing.

Gasping, Marjorie cupped her breast and offered it up higher. "More. Harder. Please, please do it harder."

Devil take it, she couldn't hold back a moment longer. Not with her heart nearly pounding out of her chest, sweat gathering at the nape of her neck, and her cunt soaking wet. Leaning forward, she kissed Marjorie fiercely, plunging her tongue into the younger woman's mouth while she tormented her tender nipple with alternate rough thumbing and firm pinches, reveling in her ward's broken cries of pleasure.

Just when Janet was about to taste that sweet pink nipple, a flash of movement in the corner of her eye made her turn her head.

Sir Lachlan!

Standing in the doorway of the solar. Watching them. His usually stoic face revealing confusion, arousal, and dismay all at the same time.

By the saints, she had done everything wrong so far. Including not informing him of Marjorie's lessons, that they had naught to do with their bedsport.

Moving her mouth to Marjorie's ear, she murmured, "My dear, it seems you did not close the door as well as you might, and we have an audience. One naughty protector. We should stop."

But the younger woman gripped her arm, her eyes heavy lidded with desire and yet an underlying desperation as well.

"*No.*"

Janet hesitated, then nodded. The only way to unravel this tangle she had created was the method she had used on countless occasions: pure brazenness. Idly tweaking Marjorie's nipple, she turned her head and met their protector's gaze. "Sir Lachlan. Come in and latch the door behind you."

Now he looked a little startled, but he obeyed her command. "Yes, my lady."

"Come here and explain yourself. I do hope you have an excellent reason for interrupting this lesson."

Sir Lachlan visibly swallowed as he moved toward the chaise, his black gaze attempting to remain on her but darting once, twice to the luscious display of Marjorie's bared breast with its taut, rosy nipple.

Well, well.

It seemed her pet wasn't nearly as indifferent to her ward as he appeared to be. This most interesting development would need to be thoroughly investigated.

At once.

• • •

He had invaded the ladies' sanctuary, so it was his own fault he'd seen what he should not: the truly erotic sight of Lady Janet and Lady Marjorie kissing on the chaise, of Lady Marjorie holding her own bared breast for her guardian to fondle.

Of course he'd seen women touch each other before. Back in the court of bachelor King James, such antics barely raised an eyebrow when wine flowed like a river. In many a tavern, too, women looking to earn extra coin would perform alluring dances together. But none of those women had ever looked like this. So passionate. So greedy for one another. These two did not play to amuse an audience or feign lust to loosen purse strings. They *wanted* this touching, no matter what Lady Janet had said about it being a lesson. And God help him, even though being replaced so soon hurt like an arrow piercing his flesh, he couldn't help but stare at the two of them, at Lady Marjorie's breast, which was a large creamy mound of perfection tipped with a swollen nipple dark pink from Lady Janet's attentions. Couldn't help the hardening of his wretched cock.

"Ladies," he said hoarsely, helplessly, when really he should have turned on his boot heel and gone, for he could not bear to witness the woman he loved falling in love with another.

Lady Janet raised an imperious brow. "You did not answer me properly. I asked you to explain your reason for interrupting this lesson, my Beast."

Now he was even more confused. Her words were brisk, as though she was irritated, and yet there was warmth in her gaze. And she'd called him "my Beast."

"Uh," he said, fumbling for the right words and failing utterly. "Forgive me. I did not know...a lesson?"

Lady Janet rose from the chaise and walked to him, then rested her hand on his chest in a gesture that both soothed and staked a claim, and his shoulders relaxed a little.

"At the king's pleasure, Marjorie will be wed to a stranger," she said calmly. "As you know, she was imprisoned in a strict convent most of her life, so she has never had the opportunity to meet young lads. She's never been kissed. Never been touched. I cannot change her past, but I can prepare her for the future. Instruct her in the ways of the marriage bed so that she is not frightened by it, here in a place that is both safe and discreet."

Put in such a way, it almost made sense. His mother probably would have championed something similar; he'd overheard her lecturing his father on many occasions about his stubborn stance on the role of young women in the clan and their lack of knowledge on worldly matters. Then she'd been killed, and any hope of his father adopting her startling and modern ideas had died with her.

Yet he couldn't halt the heartfelt words that sprang to his lips. "I am not…replaced?"

Lady Janet frowned. "I am a forthright woman. If I no longer wish to bed you, I will say it to your face. As you are free to tell me. And I most certainly desire to have you in my bed. So tell me, Sir Lachlan, are you going to continue on your merry way, or…"

"Or?" he prompted, his heart thundering in his chest.

A wicked smile curved her lips, one that made his cock throb. "Or assist me with my lesson?"

Lady Marjorie gasped, but her eyes were bright with curiosity as she shifted on the chaise. "Assist…how?"

"Yes," he echoed hesitantly. "How?"

Lady Janet caressed his chest. "I can teach my ward how to kiss, about the pleasures found in her own body. Alas, though, I cannot show her how to handle her future husband's cock. How to kiss it. Suck it. Coax it to release seed. But *you* could, with my support."

A dark thrill shot through him, and he barely suppressed a moan. How often had he dreamed of the woman he loved teasing him, ruthlessly using him for her own enjoyment? If he agreed, not only would he please his lover, he would be serving sweet Lady Marjorie as well. Two women—one he loved, one he unwillingly had tender feelings for—touching him. Instructing him.

Pleasuring him.

"Very well," he said gruffly.

Marjorie clapped her hands together, the movement lifting her bared breast higher. "You will? Oh, thank you! I am so eager to learn. I know I've only a short time to learn a lifetime's worth of knowledge before the king yanks…er, before I must leave…"

"Do not think of that, dear one," said Lady Janet. "Think of today. Think of now. We must begin without delay. Sir Lachlan, if you would remove your clothing and place your hands atop your head."

He'd never undressed faster in his life, and soon his doublet, shirt, shoes, stockings, and hose sat in a pile on the solar floor. The afternoon sun was sensually warm on his naked flesh, and he arched his back a little as he placed his hands on his head as instructed. He just hoped Lady Marjorie wasn't a swooning virgin, as much like the rest of him, his cock was large, and it was already thickening and lengthening.

"So many scars," said Lady Marjorie, biting her lip. "That fresh one…"

Before he could lower his arms and cover himself, Lady Janet placed a hand on the small of his back and rubbed in small circles. "Indeed. Each one a mark of courage, of bravery in service to the king. And the last in service to us. Each one is to be admired. Also to be admired is his exceedingly impressive cock. Take a cushion and kneel at his feet, Marjorie. Sir Lachlan has graciously allowed you to practice on him, but he may call a halt at any time. If he does so and you do not stop at once, my dear, it will be the last lesson you have. Understood?"

"Yes," said Lady Marjorie softly as she gazed up at him with wide eyes. "May I touch you, Sir Lachlan?"

God's blood, she aroused him—the curiosity, the innocence in that blue gaze, yet with kiss-swollen lips and that pretty pink nipple exposed to his avid stare. "Just Lachlan. Aye."

Very, very tentatively she reached up and brushed her fingers along his length. At the heady contrast of her cool, smooth skin, his cock jerked against his stomach, and the young woman reared back in alarm.

"Such a rampant cock!" said Lady Janet, her amusement plain. "You must take it in hand, dear one. Be firm. Show that you are in command. By the by, it is highly unlikely your future husband's manhood will be this large, so if you can master this one, you can master anything."

Lady Marjorie nodded, a rather endearing expression of determination settling on her beautiful face. This time she wrapped her fingers around his cock and squeezed gently as she leaned in to inspect the full length of him, the coarse black hair surrounding it, his heavy balls dangling underneath. Inexpertly stroking, massaging, her touch becoming more sure as she grew in confidence. Lachlan closed his eyes and began to count backward. With both women touching him, this might well be the shortest lesson in history.

"What did you say, Lachlan?" asked Lady Marjorie.

His eyes flew open. "Uh…"

Lady Janet laughed. "He is counting in Gaelic. Which means you are doing wonderfully. Now you have learned his length and girth, you might learn his taste."

Lachlan's breath caught. He would not survive this.

But what a fine, fine path to his demise.

Chapter Seven

"How are you enjoying yourself, my Beast?"

Lachlan tried to answer Lady Janet's query, but in truth he could scarcely form words. The illusion of restraint in having his hands atop his head, the sun warming his naked body, Lady Marjorie kneeling at his feet and eagerly teasing his engorged cock and balls, Lady Janet behind him, murmuring soothing words, her soft hand caressing his back in gratitude at his participation in her lesson…

Paradise.

As a young lad he'd seen the success of a dominant woman and submissive man as lovers, though his parents hadn't been wed. Deciding then he wanted that for himself, he'd been disappointed time and time again by women who expected him to demand, to enforce, to take in the bedchamber as he did on the battlefield. They'd never cared enough to ask or even tried to see into his soul and discover his true desires.

Until Lady Janet, in the Stirling Castle hallway. Again by the campfire at Loch Leven, in his bedchamber here at St. Andrews. And now in this sun-drenched sanctuary, at her command, he had not one but *two* women pleasuring him.

A truly great time to be alive.

He grunted. All the speech he could manage.

Lady Janet laughed and trailed her fingertips down to the small of his back. "I believe that was an answer of sorts. Now, Marjorie dear, kiss his cock. Take the tip in your mouth and give it a little lick. Ah, yes, clever lass. That's the way..."

He gasped, his hands tightening on his head as Lady Marjorie's little pink tongue flicked back and forth across the sensitive head of his cock. "*God's blood...*"

"Such blasphemy!" Lady Janet teased as she kissed his shoulder, then gently bit it, making him pant. "But you've been such an obedient and helpful Beast, and this requires a reward. I know you need to spend soon. Tell me, pet. Should I assist?"

"How?"

Almost idly, she caressed the hard, muscled curve of his backside. "Have you ever been touched here? The way you touched me by the campfire at the loch?"

"No," he croaked.

"Would you like to be?" she asked softly before going up on her toes and pressing her mouth to his ear. "Would you like me inside you?"

Lachlan shuddered so hard that Marjorie squeaked in protest at the disruption to her play.

"Please," he said, unashamed to beg for something he'd wanted, something he'd needed, for so long: complete and utter ownership of his body by this woman. "*Please.*"

"Very well. You'll feel wetness. My own cunt juices. I'll start with a fingertip." Janet kissed his shoulder before peering around it. "Marjorie dear, can you manage two tasks at once? I should like to watch you touch yourself while you suck Lachlan's cock."

"My shift is in the way," said Lady Marjorie uncertainly.

"Do you wish to remove it?"

The younger woman glanced at him and bit her lip. "Um…"

"I know it is awkward to be naked in front of a man for the first time," said Lady Janet. "But I feel quite confident in stating that my Beast feels as much admiration for your curves as I do. Lachlan?"

"Beautiful," he rasped. "So beautiful."

Marjorie blinked in surprise, but moments later she took a deep breath, then tugged her shift over her head and tossed it away. He couldn't help but stare at the bounty revealed: the soft, rounded lushness of her breasts and belly and hips; the tangle of brown bush covering her mound; the glimpse of delicate pink flesh between her stocking-clad thighs. It would be a fortunate husband indeed who rested his weary head on such fine pillows.

Yet as though the vision of naked perfection on her knees and kissing his cock wasn't enough to heat his blood to boiling, the next thing he heard was the rustle of fabric behind him and the rubbing of slick flesh. He couldn't see Lady Janet wetting her finger with her own honey, but he knew the exquisite clasp of that hot cunt, and just the sound of her arousal, her *purpose*, dampened the end of his cock with seed.

"Are you ready for me?" asked Lady Janet.

Only forever.

"Aye," he replied. "Please."

Her fingertips caressed his arse before delving between the cheeks to rim his back entrance, smearing it with her fragrant wetness. Then slowly, so slowly, one finger began to penetrate him. Lachlan groaned at the odd new sensation, the slight burn as she stretched him, the way his body both resisted the intrusion and teased his senses with the promise of a greater pleasure than he'd ever known. "More."

Lady Janet nipped his neck. "Did you hear that, Marjorie? My Beast wishes for more. Because he has been so obliging, we must grant his request. See if you can take his cock a little deeper in your mouth. Suck a little harder. And do not stop touching yourself."

His low roar near rattled the furniture in the solar as Lady Marjorie dutifully did as she was bidden, and Lady Janet's honey-wet finger pressed onward into his arse.

In. Out. In. Out. A rhythm, a friction to steal his wits.

"Can't…hold on…" Lachlan gritted out, his whole body shaking.

"Marjorie," said Lady Janet sharply. "Rest his cock between your breasts and squeeze it hard." As Marjorie obeyed, Janet commanded, "Lachlan, you shall anoint those sweet pink nipples with your seed. Do it. *Now.*"

With a feral snarl, Lachlan's back arched, and seed gushed from his cock onto Lady Marjorie's breasts, covering them in a pearly, sticky mess. The younger woman continued to rub herself frantically between her legs and moments later reached her own release, her sobbing cry echoing in the solar.

When he and Lady Marjorie recovered their senses, and Lady Janet carefully removed her finger from his body, they both looked at her, awaiting their next instruction.

"Lady," he said uncertainly, sure she must also need release. "You have not…"

"A truth," replied Janet, stumbling over to the chaise. "Help me undress."

Even in their post-release lethargy, he and Lady Marjorie obeyed with haste. Soon Lady Janet's hood, girdle, dark-blue gown, kirtle, and shift lay draped over large floor cushions, leaving her clad in nothing but her stockings.

She arranged herself on the chaise, spread her thighs, and trailed a slow hand down from neck to jutting nipple to glistening mound with its flaming tangle of bush. All he and

Lady Marjorie could do was watch, their gazes hungry.

"What must we do?" asked Marjorie in a hushed, reverent tone.

Janet smiled. "Lachlan is going to pleasure my cunt. Aren't you, pet?"

"Aye," he said hoarsely, gratefully kneeling between her thighs. But before she permitted him his feast, she leaned forward and tangled her fingers in his hair, plundering his mouth in a brutal, heated kiss.

"And you, Marjorie, are going to sit beside me and tend to my nipples. They are in desperate need of pinching. And sucking."

He'd not thought this day could be improved. Yet above him, as he lapped at Lady Janet's soaked cunt, Lady Marjorie attended to her guardian's taut, pale-brown nipples with the same air of curiosity and eagerness that she'd displayed for his cock. Touching. Kissing. And at last, sucking.

Lady Janet moaned. "I've not had two lovers together before. This is *heavenly*. Don't stop. Don't you dare stop…"

Lachlan glanced at Lady Marjorie, who grinned and winked at him before sucking harder on Lady Janet's nipple. Not to be outdone, he rasped his short beard across Lady Janet's inner thighs, pushed two fingers inside her cunt, and fastened his lips around her pearl. Their cool, controlled lover writhed on the chaise, but they continued to pleasure her until she threw back her head and screamed in ecstasy, grinding her cunt against Lachlan's face as release overcame her.

Licking his lips to retain the taste of Lady Janet in his mouth, Lachlan rested his head on her belly and draped his arm over her thighs. On the chaise, Lady Marjorie had pressed herself close, resting her head on her guardian's shoulder. Now this, this was heavenly.

"I suppose we must…rise soon," he mumbled. "Guests

for supper."

"Guests?" said Lady Marjorie. "What guests?"

"From the neighboring lands, those whom the king was friendly with," said Lady Janet. "I have not met them as yet."

"I have," said Lachlan. "It's the Sinclairs. Niall and Jean. And the Campbells. Hamish and Aileen."

Lady Janet froze. *"Aileen Campbell?"* she choked out. "Let me up. Let me *up.*"

Stunned, he could only watch as she dislodged herself from them and darted over to her pile of discarded clothing to pull on her shift. She was tense and upset, looking as though she wished to flee not just the solar but the manor as well.

Why would Aileen Campbell coming to supper make her react so? Were they old enemies?

The back of his neck prickled. Perchance at supper he would find out.

・・・

She held onto peace of mind by the thinnest of threads.

Taking another gulp of wine, Janet counted to ten in Gaelic, French, and Latin in her head just to suppress the bloodcurdling shriek threatening to unleash at any moment.

For in this hall, sitting just a few feet away to her right, sat ebony-haired, violet-eyed Aileen, her first lover. Her first love.

And no one else at the table knew.

Janet forced a smile as conversation flowed around her and the men and women sampled the many sweet and savory dishes the kitchens had prepared. Next to Aileen sat her beefy red-haired husband, Hamish, then Jean Sinclair, a pretty blonde. At the other end of the table was Niall Sinclair, a silver-haired diplomat. To her left were Lachlan and Marjorie, and Hamish's equally red-haired younger brother, Angus, a charming and extraordinarily well-dressed courtier she didn't trust for a moment. But try as she might, she couldn't stop herself from glancing at Aileen. Aileen couldn't stop glancing at her either.

And she *knew* that Marjorie and Lachlan had noticed something amiss. They were whispering, their foreheads nearly touching, and sending her concerned glances.

This would not be something she could brazen her way through. Not after the blissful hours they'd spent together in the solar. But she needed to speak to Aileen privately, without any of the other guests growing suspicious. Or guessing their truth.

"What on earth are you two whispering about, Sir Lachlan? Do share it with the table," said Jean Sinclair with a friendly smile.

Lachlan went rigid in his seat, his cheeks darkening a little. "Nothing of importance."

The older blond woman laughed. "Nonsense. You both looked quite serious. Are you and Lady Marjorie sweethearts?"

Marjorie sent her an anxious glance. Lachlan's expression settled into impassiveness, a sure sign that he did not wish to be questioned. In truth, this afternoon the three of them had become lovers. While in the past she would have paraded her latest lover about, she didn't want to reveal that tidbit to these courtiers. It was too new. Too complex. Too precious.

Janet cleared her throat. "Lady Marjorie is my ward until the king selects a husband for her, and Sir Lachlan was appointed to protect us both. More wine, Jean?"

"You are fortunate, Lady Janet, to have so fair a maiden under your roof," said Angus Campbell, raising his goblet to both her and Lady Marjorie. "We are starved of beauty and overrun with scholars and monks in St. Andrews."

Aileen shook her head at her husband's brother. "Starved

of beauty? Jean and I are thrilled to learn we are gargoyles, Angus. But you are right. Beauty has arrived, and we should rejoice."

As though a cord about her neck tugged at her, Janet met Aileen's soft, yielding yet heated gaze. Saints alive, she played a dangerous game with her husband sitting next to her!

"Mistress Campbell," said Lachlan abruptly. "You know Lady Janet?"

Oh no.

Hamish Campbell raised a bushy red eyebrow at his wife. "You did not say so, sweetheart."

"Ah…from a very long time ago," said Aileen, her smile strained. "One summer we—"

"Shared a French tutor," said Lady Janet crisply before her former lover wilted under questioning and hurt those at the table. Only both sets of parents knew the real reason for Aileen's swift marriage to Hamish and Janet being gifted to the king. "The worst in history. Half of every lesson, he grumbled about all Scotland's faults compared to France. Too cold! Too rainy! And the food, *mon dieu*!"

Aileen laughed, her shoulders visibly relaxing. "I always wondered why he did not leave if it was all so terrible."

"Maybe debts in France," said Niall.

"A cellar full of dismembered limbs," said Angus, his eyes glinting.

Hamish glared at his brother. "There are ladies present."

"No ordinary ladies, brother! Most interesting ones. Especially Lady Janet, here. Revered the length and breadth of the country as—"

"*Proudly* the worst sinner in Scotland," said Lady Janet archly, not at all inclined to hear false flattery. "It shall be a sad day when I am forced to relinquish the title. I do so enjoy turning the menfolk's hair white."

Lachlan lifted his wine goblet. "Long may you reign."

She winked at him and raised her own. "To mischief and mayhem."

The others at the table added their salute. "To mischief and mayhem!"

Niall then frowned. "But not too much. Those south of the border are ever ready to invade. Sir Lachlan, you have fought in many battles. Would you say the threat remains?"

Janet hesitated, torn at the turn in conversation. While she was greatly relieved to no longer have all gazes on her and knew without looking that her former lover felt the same, Lachlan hated to speak in public. He'd always been the one who lurked in the shadows, the man of deeds rather than words. The only person he'd felt comfortable talking with for any length of time was the king.

Indeed, Lachlan appeared to be wishing himself miles away.

"Aye," he said eventually. "Always will."

"But we have an English-born queen now," said Angus. "Surely you are overcautious."

Janet snorted. "Time will tell where Margaret's true loyalties lie. Her Tudor blood flows strong."

"When there is a Scots prince in the cradle, we'll all feel better," said Jean. "'Tis a woman's most sacred duty, after all. None more so than a queen."

"Indeed," Janet replied, gritting her teeth. Now it was she who wished to flee into the night. Each day she thought she'd finally accepted her barrenness. Then a woman would comment on pregnancy or childbirth, and it would sting like a thousand little cuts.

"More wine, lady?" said Lachlan, an understanding in his gaze that made her heart clench.

"I believe I will," she replied softly.

"Before you do, Lady Janet," burst out Aileen. "I am feeling a little unwell. Do you have some peppermint tonic, by chance?"

She hesitated, torn. They did need to talk. And yet somehow leaving the table with Aileen, in a sense choosing her over Lachlan and Marjorie, felt like a betrayal after everything that had happened on the journey from Stirling Castle and since they'd arrived.

Do I still desire Aileen?

Janet studied her former lover. She was indeed an attractive woman. But it had been so long, and she'd had so many lovers since. Besides. She wasn't Marjorie, with luscious, plump curves, bright-blue eyes, and a smile like sunshine. Or brawny, gruff, deliciously obedient Lachlan. Maybe now it was time to lay the past to rest forever.

"I do," she replied, turning to the others but truly addressing Lachlan and Marjorie. "Please excuse us just for a few minutes while I assist Aileen."

They walked from the room, and she directed Aileen into a small antechamber next to the chapel that served as a storage room of sorts, without a tonic to be found.

"Janet…" Aileen said huskily, reaching for her.

She stepped back. "It's been a long time."

"What is the matter? You still want me. I know you do. We couldn't take our eyes off one another at supper."

Janet shook her head. "I was shocked to see you. I did not know you and Hamish were the longstanding guests of the king. But I do not dally with those who are wed. An unbreakable rule of mine."

The other woman pouted. "You and your rules. Do not think of my husband; we have an understanding now that he has his heirs. Think of me. Think of us and all that time lost because of my silly father. I never stopped loving you."

"No, Aileen," she murmured. "That summer will always hold a special place in my heart. But a memory it shall remain."

"Is it the king's Beast? Or your ward?" Aileen said abruptly, her violet eyes flashing with jealousy. "I saw the tender look you gave her."

"Do not—"

"You'll forget Lady Marjorie once she's wed, and I'll be waiting. I'll win back your love, and it will be just like before; you'll see."

Dismay gathered like storm clouds. They could not tarry in this room any longer, or the other guests would grow curious. But it seemed her former lover was determined to recapture the past no matter what she was told…an act that could unleash several kinds of trouble.

And more trouble was the last thing she needed.

· · ·

Everything had been so right. And now it was all wrong.

Marjorie stared at the duck, beef, and cooked vegetables on her pewter plate, her appetite gone since Janet had left the room with Aileen Campbell. She and Lachlan had seen there was some sort of bond between the two women—he'd even asked if they knew each other—but she didn't believe for a moment the story about sharing a tutor. Two people did not share stolen glances over a *tutor*. And that made her heart hurt.

Their time in the wagon and in the solar with Lachlan had meant everything. She'd thought Janet felt something for her in return. But maybe that was just the loneliness that had been her most faithful companion, tricking her, seeing something that wasn't there.

Angus Campbell cleared his throat. "I am desperate for some air. Lady Marjorie, would you care to walk in the gardens for a bit? I should enjoy hearing of your convent life."

"Sun is setting," growled Lachlan before she could reply.

"Nonsense," said Angus. "Plenty of time for a short walk. No need to scowl, Sir Lachlan. You know, if you scowled less and smiled more, you might find a wife as pretty as Mistress Sinclair here."

Lachlan glared at him. "Not looking."

Not looking.

Marjorie winced. Just two words and her heart had crushed to powder.

The second rejection shouldn't hurt; she wasn't free to choose Lachlan even if she wished to. But it did. Especially after Janet had chosen Aileen. Especially when in the solar she had touched him so intimately, had him in her mouth, reveled in the splash of his seed on her breasts.

It seemed no matter what she said or did, she would always be unwanted.

"Lady Marjorie? A walk?"

She studied Angus Campbell. The man appeared her opposite in every way: slender, handsome, red hair falling to his shoulders without a single strand out of place. His clothing was new, costly, and in the French style. In truth, he did not make her heart beat faster like Lachlan did—or Janet, for that matter. And his elaborate flattery seemed to extend to all women rather than her in particular—a true courtier. Yet no one else had asked her to take a walk in the garden nearby, and in her guardian's absence, Jean Sinclair clearly approved. She was smiling indulgently at the notion of her accompanying Angus.

Could she grow to love such a man, one already in the king's favor?

There was only one way to be sure.

"Yes," Marjorie said abruptly. "I should like that, Master Campbell. The flowers in the garden are lovely."

"Not as lovely as you," he replied gallantly, rising to his feet.

Lachlan snorted, and she ignored it completely. Hearing a waterfall of compliments might go a way to mending her bruised heart.

Outside, the sun had begun to set, bathing the manor in a pretty pinkish glow. Insects and birds chirped merrily, and the closer they moved to the well-tended gardens, the stronger the scent of blooms became. In truth she preferred the fresh scent of herbs, especially the peppermint the women had washed her hair with, but flowers were quite nice also.

"So," said Angus, offering his arm. "Tell me of yourself. Oh, and mind my doublet sleeve; it is satin and newly arrived from Paris."

Marjorie sighed inwardly. She would have to become accustomed to such warnings; many of the men at court took as much care with their clothing as ladies and only wore rich, colorful fabrics from Paris or Rome. "There is little to tell, sir," she said slowly. "I lived most of my life in a convent, until the king in his mercy brought me to court and placed me in the care of Lady Janet, for which I am most grateful."

"Really? A gentle lady like yourself would find her coarse, surely."

"Not at all," she replied firmly. "I have found her most kind and generous."

Especially in lessons of a lusty nature.

Angus chuckled. "Your loyalty is commendable. An admirable trait in a wife, alongside a handsome dowry. Such a shame your traitor father's lands belong to the crown now."

Marjorie halted, looking up at the man in disbelief. "Beg pardon?"

He smiled ruefully. "Forgive me. I misspoke. Do you embroider? Play an instrument?"

"I enjoy embroidery," she said stiffly. "It is starting to get dark. We should return to the hall."

"How *unfriendly*," Angus scolded, stepping closer so he

loomed over her. "Does the king know how ill mannered you are? How cold? Do not fret, Marjie. I shall warm you."

Before she could inform him she neither required warming nor appreciated her name being shortened so, Angus slid his hands to either side of her face and kissed her.

She felt…nothing.

Well, nothing but anger at this stranger handling her without permission and disgust at the slimy tongue attempting to gain entry to her mouth. Janet had spoken of pleasure for all, of not forcing your will on another. Clearly this man had not received the correct guidance. Lifting her hands, she pressed them against his chest in an attempt to push him away.

"There, there," Angus muttered, kissing a wet trail to her ear. "I know you are virgin and quite overcome with my skill. Do not worry; I shall teach you…*ow*! My foot!"

Marjorie stepped back. Really, she needed a cloth to wipe him from her face, but her gown sleeve would have to suffice. "You are fortunate my eating knife is in the hall, sir."

His eyes narrowed, his cheeks bright red. "Fat as a sow and ugly as well. Who would want to wed you anyway? I am far superiorrrrrrrrrahhhhhh…"

In the blink of an eye, Angus was jerked away and slammed into a tree trunk.

"What did you say?" snarled Lachlan, the sound of his meaty fist tearing the other man's satin doublet, newly arrived from Paris, far more satisfying than she would ever confess.

"Naught! Put me down! I am friend to King James!"

Marjorie folded her arms. She had become a terrible person. At Stirling Castle, the sight of Lachlan punishing another man for bad behavior had alarmed her. Now, she rather liked it. If he continued holding Angus just so, she could probably land a few kicks to the shin in retribution for that slimy tongue. But darkness was encroaching rapidly, and it would be difficult to explain this without causing Janet embarrassment.

"Lachlan," she said softly. "Let him go."

"He *insulted* you."

"I know. And he will have a sore foot and ruined doublet to show for it. He is not worth your further effort. Or mine."

The Beast growled at Angus but let him drop to the grass in a heap. "Run, rabbit. To return…is to be hunted."

The other man went whiter than snow, scrambled to his feet, and hurried back toward the manor.

"Thank you, once again, for your assistance. I did not want to say it in front of that snake, but you already angered the king because of me. I should not like to see you in trouble."

Lachlan puffed out a short breath and flexed his fingers. "Did he hurt you?"

"No. But he kissed me, and I did not want him to. Oh, Lachlan, it was awful. I called him snake because of his slimy tongue. He put it in my ear! Ugh!"

"Lady Marjorie—"

"Just Marjorie," she said swiftly. "We might not be sweethearts, but after today I think we are becoming friends?"

Lachlan looked to the heavens, but when he gazed at her again, the tender heat in his eyes burned her. "Good friends."

A sob caught in her throat, and she flung herself at his chest. When his arms slowly closed around her and one hand rubbed her back, she burrowed against his warmth. "I…I do not wish to leave here. To wed a stranger. I want to stay with you and Janet. I like you both. So very much."

"Aye." His arms tightened, his lips brushing her forehead in the briefest of caresses that branded her for eternity.

Yet they both well knew when the time came…

Staying would not be a choice.

Chapter Eight

After several days of biting winds and just enough rain to trap everyone inside the manor until they paced like caged animals, to see the clouds had cleared and naught more than a gentle breeze stirred the trees was a great relief.

Lachlan waited at the bottom of the stairs for Marjorie and Lady Janet, at his feet one basket with food and flagons of wine and small ale and another with an old woolen blanket and several cushions. They were all in need of some sunshine and fresh air after the foul weather, but more especially, time alone together. Lady Janet had been furious when she'd learned of Angus Campbell's behavior in the garden and had forbidden the man from visiting the manor again. She had offered reassurance regarding her absence with Aileen Campbell, yet there remained an air of tension about her. He hoped in a less formal setting, she might confide what weighed on her mind.

"Do I see wine in that basket?"

He smiled as Lady Janet descended the staircase like an empress. Well. Empress of his world, at least. "Aye, lady.

Enough for merriment."

"Excellent," said Marjorie, trailing just behind. "Where are you taking us, Lachlan? Are we riding?"

"No need. It's a short distance. Half mile or so."

Lady Janet nodded. "Lead on, then. If I'm trapped one more moment within these walls, I shall go mad. I always find a walk helps to clear my mind."

It was tempting to press her further, but servants were bustling about, equally eager to make use of the fine weather and complete their tasks before chapel. Some had been given leave to visit their families for the afternoon and moved particularly swiftly with baskets of linens to be laundered, silver to be polished, and rugs to be beaten free of dust and dirt.

Instead, he, Lady Janet, and Marjorie made their way down the gravel path, past the flower garden and orchard, toward the hunting grounds. When they reached a large clump of shrubbery, he directed the ladies to the right, down a narrow way that had been gouged out of a bank to allow access to the stream below.

"Here," said Lachlan, leading them to a small sand clearing about twenty feet wide and deep. "Thought this might do."

"Oh, it's lovely," said Marjorie, clasping her hands together.

Eager to serve, he unpacked the first basket, spreading out the rug and arranging the cushions in a half circle. Lady Janet sank onto the rug with a deep sigh, leaning back on a cushion and lifting her face to the sun.

"I'll need all the lemon juice in Scotland for the freckles I shall gain this day, but it will be worth it. Hold your noses now, I'm removing my shoes and stockings."

As soon as she did so, Marjorie began to cough and sway before pressing her hand to her forehead, swooning onto the cushion and twitching, then lying deathly still.

Lachlan applauded.

Lady Janet raised an eyebrow. "*Saucy*. Both of you."

"Are you going to punish us, mistress?" said Marjorie, batting her lashes, and her guardian couldn't help but smile.

"Indeed. An extra half hour on your knees—"

"Hooray!"

"In chapel."

They both stared at her in horror. Lady Janet stared back for a few moments, then she began to laugh. "Your *faces*."

The sound warmed his heart, as did the easy way she lounged. God's blood, he wished he could declare his heart, but it never seemed to be quite the right time, and he had no wish to make a fool of himself. Instead, Lachlan unpacked the second basket and poured a goblet of wine for each of them. Soon they lay together in companionable silence, the sound of birds chirping and water trickling over ancient rocks enough.

Eventually, Marjorie sat up. "Will you tell us a story from court, Janet? A *bawdy* one?"

Lady Janet held out her goblet to be refilled. "A bawdy tale? From me? Impossible, my dear. I have led a quiet and scandal-free life…that wasn't a snort, was it Lachlan?"

"Noooo, my lady," he replied, unable to halt his lips twitching.

"It *was*," she said archly. "For that you may rub my feet. And I'll tell you a tale of the time I found a French envoy fucking an English border lord in a privy closet. France had England tamed and well conquered, I assure you…"

Soothed by her husky tone, Lachlan settled into his task and circled one thumb into the arch of her foot. Lady Janet had a gift for storytelling; the detail she remembered, alongside her sharp wit and her ability to mimic voices of certain courtiers, amused him to no end.

Some events he recalled, like the occasion she and James had a particularly hot-tempered argument. She'd hurled a goblet—missing the king by several feet at least—which instead flew straight out a window and knocked unconscious a hapless guard taking a piss against the wall. James had sworn he was done with her, a threat which lasted all of an hour. Though they had ceased to be lovers some years prior, all of Scotland knew she remained close to the king's heart.

At one point his thigh was nudged, and he glanced down to see a small foot before glancing up to see Marjorie's hopeful smile. He wordlessly shuffled across the rug a little so she could rest her foot on his leg before using his other thumb to rub her instep.

Like this, it was easy to pretend they were both his ladies, unlikely as the dream might be.

"I am getting parched," said Lady Janet. "It is time for someone else to tell a tale. Lachlan?"

His gut twisted. "Nay," he said swiftly, refilling her goblet again. "You have the gift."

She smiled, took a few sips of wine, and launched into a recollection of James and Margaret's wedding feast the previous year at Edinburgh. Or rather, the antics after the king and queen had retired.

Marjorie's eyes grew as round as pewter plates as she unsuccessfully attempted to stifle her laughter. "Sword fighting...*naked*?"

Lady Janet nodded. "Indeed. But then an English envoy cut his leg, so the swords were put to one side. They decided to instead measure their cocks at full mast to declare the winner. 'Tis fortunate the wedding was held in August rather than December; otherwise a thumb might have triumphed."

"Clearly, Lachlan did not compete," said Marjorie, her cheeks pink.

"Duties elsewhere," he replied, his own cheeks burning.

Lady Janet raised her goblet in a salute. "You are admirably dedicated to duty, just like I am admirably dedicated to finishing my wine and resting on this cushion while someone else speaks. My throat is protesting. Lachlan, I'm sure you have many bawdy stories you could tell. All those evenings spent in taverns with the king…"

He did. Probably hundreds. Yet even the thought of attempting such a feat with his affliction made cold sweat gather at the back of his neck. Only his mother and the king had accepted the flaw without judgment or scorn. His tongue refused to work when he tried to string together more than four words. It was like his mouth became separated from the rest of his body, a deserter who refused to follow orders.

"Naught of interest," he said eventually. "Shall we eat? I'll go rinse…my hands."

Both women stared at him as he got to his feet, heads tilted and eyes sharp.

Plague take it. Had they guessed?

He fled to the stream.

• • •

Confused and troubled by Lachlan's sudden departure, Marjorie glanced at Janet. "He, ah, really does not wish to speak."

Janet's brow furrowed. "No, he doesn't. And I don't believe for a moment it is any reluctance for the topic. Lachlan is no prude and knows how I am. He also knows you aren't nearly as innocent as you look."

A giggle escaped. "That is the truth. Lachlan doesn't speak very much ever, though. Only a few words at a time."

Her gaze sharpened. "Always only a few words at a time. Any more and he pauses. I wonder…" Janet tapped her chin, then raised her voice. "Lachlan! Do come back, my pet."

Their protector returned from the stream like a man who'd walked the entire length of Scotland, his steps heavy and shoulders stooped. His gaze wary. "Yes?"

Janet patted the ground beside her. "Come sit by me a moment. Then we'll eat."

Lachlan obeyed but with obvious reluctance. That, and a hint of panic in his dark eyes. Knowing Janet was probably about to ask him a very difficult question, Marjorie sat down beside him and rested her head on his shoulder, twining her fingers with his. His hand felt cold from the stream water, but it soon warmed, and she almost cheered when his fingers briefly squeezed back.

"Lachlan, my pet," said Janet, her tone unusually gentle. "I'm going to ask a rather personal question. Of course you are free to refuse, but I hope you will answer."

"Ask," he replied stiffly.

"Does it hurt for you to speak? I mean, more than a few words and your mouth hurts? Maybe an old injury?"

Lachlan went rigid, now more like a cornered Beast, his gaze darting between them as though searching for escape. "No."

Bolder than she'd ever been in her life, Marjorie said softly, "We know your mind is swift and sharp. How else would you be such a magnificent warrior? But maybe…your mouth is slower? In my mind I run like a Thoroughbred. But everything bounces, and my knees hurt, and I move more like that cursed wagon. It is terribly frustrating."

He stared at the rug, his free hand gripping his thigh so hard his knuckles were white.

"I have…a speech affliction," Lachlan rasped eventually, his gaze remaining resolutely down. "Words get stuck in m-my mouth. I know…I know what I w-want to s-say. But it does n-not *work*. Since I was a boy. The k-king knows. No one else. I say little. I pause. So they d-do not laugh. What man cannot *speak*?"

Janet reached out and grasped his chin, forcing him to look at her. "Heed me well, Lachlan. The king assigned you as protector, but I *choose* to have you as a companion. You have proven in deeds, on countless occasions, that you are a man of great courage, loyalty, and skill. A man of great character. An exemplary lover. I understand you will always be aware of your battle scars. And your speech. But neither of those things changes how I feel about you. Not one bit. You are the Highland Beast. My pet."

He shuddered, staring at Janet. Then he turned and looked at Marjorie, and the rawness of old shame, the burgeoning hope in his glistening eyes, struck her to the core. Those were emotions she knew all too well.

Marjorie beamed at him before kissing his cheek. Janet curled against his other side, and they held him tightly, stroking his hair, murmuring words of praise for sharing his painful secret with them. Gradually Lachlan began to relax, and they nudged him down onto the cushion and covered him with their bodies. He shuddered again, and a brawny arm slid around each of them, clamping them to his chest.

How long they lay together like that—with the warmth of the early-afternoon sun on their faces, the only sounds the stream and a few birds—she could not say.

Well, the only sounds except for her stomach. Mortified, Marjorie pressed on it, but naturally, it let out a second gurgle more like a thunderclap. "Do forgive me."

Lachlan slowly sat up. "I must feed you b-both. *Both*."

"What is in the basket?" asked Janet.

"Bread. Cheese. Apple tarts. A dish of berries."

Somehow, the simple meal was the best she'd tasted, and Marjorie sighed in bliss as they finished all the food and the last of the wine.

Abruptly, Janet laughed. "My dear, you have a spot of

berry juice on your chin. Let me assist you."

She lifted her chin, thinking Janet would wipe it away with her thumb. Instead, her guardian cupped her cheek, flicking the spot with her tongue before kissing her deeply. A jolt ran through her body, centering between her legs, and she moaned.

Lachlan watched them, his gaze glittering. "The sun is overwarm. We should return indoors."

"Agreed," said Janet wickedly. "My ward requires further lessons. She must learn how it feels to have a man's tongue on her pearl and in her cunt. Also, she should observe me riding my lover until he bucks like a stallion."

"Until his lover…screams with p-pleasure."

Excited beyond words, Marjorie put on her stockings and shoes before scrambling to her feet. "I'm ready."

When Janet had put on her stockings and shoes, they repacked the baskets and returned to the manor at a much brisker pace than they had left it. Nothing needed to be said; they all had the same purpose in mind. The solar and its sturdy chaise.

But when they reached the front door, a servant met them there, holding a missive.

"Letter came while you were out, mistress," he said, bowing respectfully. "From Stirling Castle."

As though all three had been doused in icy water, they froze.

"Thank you," said Janet, her smile forced. "You may go."

Once the servant had left them, Janet took the small eating knife attached to her girdle and slid the blade under the red sealing wax. Then she unfolded the parchment and began to read. When her face went gray and she pressed a hand to her breast, Marjorie's heart plummeted.

"What does it say?" she choked out.

"The king?" growled Lachlan.

Janet shook her head, her expression grim. "Nay. Queen Margaret. Come with me into the chapel."

Nausea roiled in Marjorie's stomach as they walked into the cool, dark sanctuary of the manor chapel, and for a moment she thought she would retch onto the floor. It clearly wasn't a letter advising of a visit or a summons; her guardian looked far too angry.

"What does the letter say?" she asked again, swallowing hard. Desperate not to hear the words she feared most.

"Tell us, lady," said Lachlan, even as he took Marjorie's hand and squeezed it.

"Her Grace writes," Janet bit out, "that she has heard of Lady Marjorie Hepburn's intemperate behavior toward a gentleman of good standing and knows in her heart that it is time for the king's ward to wed so a husband might lead her back to virtue and grace. To strengthen the English alliance, it is hereby decreed Lady Marjorie Hepburn shall wed the English border baron, Lord Seaton, at Carlisle two weeks hence. Preparations are being made for travel."

Marjorie's legs buckled, a wail of despair unleashing from her throat.

"Please," she begged, tears pouring down her face as she let go of Lachlan's hand and threw herself at Janet's feet. "Please do not let them take me away."

...

She might be struck down for blasphemy in a chapel, but damn the queen. Damn men who decided a woman's future with no care for her wishes. Damn that sniveling peacock Angus Campbell, who had scurried to court to whine when his pitiful attempt at seduction hadn't succeeded.

Janet sucked in a deep breath, a futile attempt at calming her rage so she might return to a place of rational reason. So she might *think*.

After that wretched dinner where Aileen had unexpectedly appeared back in her life and declared a desire to rekindle their past, she'd been quite out of sorts. But this, this was beyond all. Despite her best efforts at keeping emotionally distant from her ward, this terrible letter and Marjorie's distress were tearing her heart in two. Under no circumstances would she allow her to be snatched away because of a foolish child-queen and scorned male courtier. Certainly not to wed an *Englishman*, who would be utterly unworthy of such a treasure.

Crouching down, Janet cupped Marjorie's tearstained face and blotted the moisture with her thumbs. Then she grasped her chin firmly and kissed her. "As I said to Lachlan earlier this day, heed me well."

Marjorie sniffled, her shoulders still shaking. "Y-yes?"

"I will think of a way to stop this, dear one. But you must rise from the floor and cease your tears so I can pace and ponder. Lachlan, help her onto a chair."

Their protector scooped Marjorie from the floor, but rather than placing her on the chair, he sat down and settled her in his lap. She buried her face in his chest, her shoulders gradually shaking less and less.

Janet nodded approvingly at his tender care and began to march from one end of the chapel to the other, her heels overloud on the stone floor. "Good. Good. Now, let me see…"

It took every bit of her will to show only command and control, for the task ahead was near impossible. To defy the Queen of Scotland's decree and save Marjorie from the marital clutches of an ancient, pox-ridden English baron could be argued treasonous.

At best, she faced losing both her lovers.

At worst, she could forfeit all she had, including her own freedom.

"Do we run?" asked Lachlan, his voice low and tense.

Janet rubbed her hand across her face. "No. To run is to become a fugitive, to add abduction of the king's ward to offenses against the crown for defying a royal decree, and add a bounty on our heads from both the Scottish and English purses. We would be hunted, imprisoned, possibly killed, and Marjorie dragged back to wed the border lord."

"I don't know what t-to do," he bit out, frustration and helplessness for once transparent on his face. "I can fight. I can kill. Both skills useless here. James willnae gainsay Margaret. A border alliance w-will suit him. Even our names t-to a petition…n-no help. Plague take it!"

About to join Lachlan in unleashing every curse she knew, Janet came to an abrupt halt as one of her lover's words pounded in her mind.

Name.

Lady Janet Fraser could protest, but it would make no difference at all against the queen's decree. Sir Lachlan Ross, however, a man, or more specifically a bachelor…had something quite different to offer.

His name. His hand in marriage.

Janet hurried over to where they sat, then reached down and took their hands in each of hers. "Lachlan. Marjorie. There might be a way. But it is a plan fraught with risk."

"Tell me," said Marjorie hoarsely. "I'll do anything. Please."

"If you were wedded and bedded in the eyes of the law, how could you marry an Englishman?"

"There is no time. I am to go to Carlisle two weeks hence. The banns must be read in church for three!"

Janet gripped her hand tighter. "I did not say in the eyes of the church, dear one. I said the eyes of the *law*."

Lachlan sucked in a breath, and she knew he understood to what she referred. Scotland had forever rebelled and forged its own path, and the law in regard to marriage was one of those rebellions. While there were the usual weddings in church with a priest and posting of the banns, three kinds of irregular marriages were also valid. The first, a couple could declare themselves married in front of witnesses. The second, they could make a written promise or spoken oath of marriage, followed by a bedding. The third, a couple could present themselves as wed in public—marriage by habit and repute.

It would be unfair to ask servants or friends to be part of a plot against the crown, and for Marjorie to go about in public presenting herself as a wife would only spark a swift vengeance. But a written promise and a bedding done in secret, then revealed at the right moment...

"How can I be wed if not in church?" said Marjorie, biting her lip. "I don't understand."

"An *irregular* marriage," said Lachlan slowly.

"Exactly," said Janet. "A man and a woman consent to be wed, and so it is done. My late husband explained it to me once because lawmakers and clergymen were forever having heated debates about it. But no matter the protests from the church, irregular marriages continue to be legal. They are especially helpful in isolated places without a priest, or to protect young women from unscrupulous men making false promises just to bed them. A willing man—"

"Me."

Marjorie's head jerked as she looked up at him. Then she shook it. "I cannot ask that of you, Lachlan. You're already in trouble for killing Lord Kerr and rough-handling Master Campbell because of me. This is...this is almost treasonous. Isn't it, Janet?"

"It could be so argued," she admitted reluctantly. "Defying a royal decree, the king's ward marrying without permission, and upsetting the English also. As I said, it is fraught with risk. But if you are wedded and bedded, there is a very small chance they might allow the marriage to stand."

"You aren't asking. I'm offering," said Lachlan gruffly. "I know…I have little. No castle or fortune. N-no handsome face. I'll never read p-poetry. Or dance. But I would p-protect you…til my last b-breath. Care for you. Be loyal unto you."

Janet looked away, unable to bear the halting sweetness of the words or the sickening churn of terror and jealousy and despair in her stomach. If her plan failed, it could well send Lachlan to the stocks or a dungeon. If it succeeded, they would leave her forever and start a new family, a new life without her. As she'd already said to Aileen, she did not dally with those who were wed.

Either way, the only plan she could think of had the power to hurt her unbearably.

Holding her breath, she waited for her ward's answer.

"You are the very best of men," said Marjorie after what seemed like a hundred years of silence, cupping her hands around Lachlan's face and kissing his cheek. "Kind and generous and far more than I deserve. Yes, Sir Lachlan Ross, I consent to wed you."

Janet closed her eyes briefly. Then she forced the necessary words to her lips. "Ride to St. Andrews, to the university. There is a lawyer there, Master Shaw. Tell him the fiery one sent you, and he will assist with the proper declaration. Insist on two copies to take away with you. Do *not* speak to anyone else. This must remain a secret."

"Lady…" said Lachlan.

She halted his words with a fierce kiss, then stepped back. "Go. Go now."

And her heart shattered.

Chapter Nine

He was a married man.

Lachlan slapped his heels against Storm's flanks, urging him to gallop even faster along the road from St. Andrews back to the manor, as though pace could help him outrun his thoughts.

But nothing could change two facts. First, his new wife, Lady Marjorie Ross, clung to his back, and in Storm's saddlebags were two signed and sealed documents attesting to that. Second, he had utterly betrayed his longtime friend King James, the only man who had judged him on deeds and character rather than learning or speech or appearance. The man who had raised him high.

God's blood. He knew he'd done the right thing wedding Marjorie, a woman he liked, admired, and lusted for. But a future of great uncertainty loomed: what would happen when James and Margaret discovered their defiance of a royal decree and arranged border-alliance marriage? Would he be imprisoned and Marjorie forced to wed the Englishman anyway? How would their legal union affect Lady Janet—not just his lover but the woman he loved?

His wedding day should be a happy one. Instead, his stomach churned and sweat dampened his body, sensations he'd only experienced before on the eve of a great battle.

As they approached the gate to the manor—not the main gate, but a rear one that led to the vast hunting grounds—he slowed Storm to a trot. A burly guard stepped out of the box, and Lachlan could feel Marjorie's heightened tension as she gripped his waist tighter.

"Sir Lachlan!" hailed the guard. "Lady Marjorie. I was not aware you had left the manor."

"An errand," said Lachlan stiffly.

"Of what nature?"

Behind him, Marjorie laughed—a high, forced sound. "Oh, sir, 'tis my fault entirely. I am a silly woman who desired the tang of sea air in her lungs more than anything on this earth, and I pleaded with Sir Lachlan to take me to town. I believe he did so just so he would not hear my voice a moment more."

Lachlan held his breath, but the guard relaxed, his lips twitching.

"My mother loves to watch the fishing boats. I don't know why. Come in, then, but remember to inform the guardhouse if you are leaving so we know where you are."

"Aye," said Lachlan, nodding as they rode through the gate. With Storm at full gallop again, they crossed the hunting grounds in no time at all, then approached the stables at a brisk trot.

Even before the stable boy had a chance to come out and take the reins, Lachlan swung down onto the ground and swiftly moved the precious marriage documents from the saddlebag to be concealed under his doublet.

Then he reached up for Marjorie. "Home, lady wife," he rasped.

"Thank you, husband," she whispered in his ear, and as he helped her down from Storm's back, he had to fight down a surprising rush of emotion at the word. *Husband.*

Despite everything, it sounded good.

They walked in silence to the manor front door, and his gaze darted left and right, fully expecting to be ambushed at any moment. While he trusted the discretion of the silver-bearded lawyer, Master Shaw—distant kin to Lady Janet and possessing a loathing of all Tudors, whom he called upstart usurpers of the Plantagenet throne—others at the university could have recognized them.

Lachlan halted at the foot of the stairs. "What do you wish to d-do?"

Marjorie visibly swallowed, her face pale, and he thought he might know her mind. Lawful completion of their marriage declaration required a bedding, the sooner the better. It was no wonder she appeared as skittish as a newborn colt.

"Could we...could we possibly step into the chapel for a moment?" she asked hesitantly. "I should like to pray. To confess. And to ask for God's blessing."

"As you like."

Hurrying to the altar, Marjorie then knelt on a purple velvet cushion in front of it and crossed herself. When she raised an imperious eyebrow at Lachlan, he reluctantly dropped to his knees beside her. Give him a battlefield over a holy place of worship any day.

"If I am struck b-by lightning...'tis your fault," he growled.

His wife made a noise that sounded much like a hastily suppressed laugh. Then she clasped her hands together. "Bless us, Heavenly Father, for we have sinned. Er...quite a serious one. Defied the decree of your anointed sovereign's wife and wed without permission. An irregular marriage without priest or banns. Ah, please do forgive us for that. We mean no harm or malice. But I'm sure you understand that I cannot wed an Englishman, for *obvious* reasons…"

Lachlan was far less successful in suppressing his levity, but Marjorie elbowed him sharply in the ribs and he grunted in discomfort.

"As I was *saying*," she continued, "I could not wed an Englishman. But I consented to wed Sir Lachlan Ross instead. He is the best of men. Good and loyal and so kind to me. I am most fortunate. And he consented to wed me. Tell Him, Lachlan."

"Aye, I consented. With a free and g-glad heart," he said, solemn now, and Marjorie leaned over and rubbed her cheek against his like a kitten. Again he swallowed hard against a rush of emotion. He'd wed a good woman, at least. One who liked him in return, was affectionate, and accepted his faults and flaws. In other circumstances he would have been happy indeed.

Marjorie took a deep breath and raised her gaze to the roof. "Now we must go upstairs, and, ah, well…you know. So we ask thy blessing and humbly beseech thee for a *long* and… er…fruitful union. Amen."

"Amen," he echoed.

"Thank you," she said as they got to their feet before leaving the chapel. "I know it is foolish—"

"It is not," he said firmly.

Fortunately the servants were busy with preparations for supper and weren't paying close attention to them. They climbed the stairs in silence, but the closer they got to Marjorie's chamber, the more her steps faltered. When she pushed open her door, her hand visibly shook.

Lachlan grimaced in sympathy. In truth, this was the first time in hours that something felt wrong. Even after what they'd done in the solar, she would still have a virgin's anxiety, and he didn't know exactly what to say to reassure her. Lady

Janet would. She always knew what to say, especially in regard to lusty matters. But she was away in her own chamber.

"I wish Janet were here," Marjorie blurted before staring at him in horror. "Forgive me. That was beyond awful. After your noble sacrifice, I didn't mean...I just—"

"I wish the same," he said simply, choosing to be as honest as she had been, for she deserved such respect. "It feels...wrong without her."

Her shoulders sagged. "I want to be bedded by you. I do. I care for you so very much, and I know you will make it as nice as possible. But I would be less anxious if Janet watched and instructed me."

A flame lit inside him, one that made his cock jerk. "Watched and instructed *us*."

Marjorie licked her lips, her eyes darkening to pure sapphire. "We should go and find the mistress of the manor, then, husband."

He bowed. "As you desire, lady wife."

• • •

Marjorie and Lachlan were consummating their marriage, and she had only her ever-faithful companion: wine.

Janet took another gulp from her goblet and stared out the window of her bedchamber, watching the shadows lengthen in the late-afternoon sun.

The day had started so promisingly with the jaunt to the stream. How pleasant it had been to relax with her lovers, laugh and tell bawdy tales, and eat delicious food outside in the secluded spot. When Lachlan had shared his secret, a new tenderness and protectiveness for him had rushed through her. But when they had returned to the manor...

She shuddered. A dark chasm had opened, threatening to swallow her at any time. From the moment Lachlan and

Marjorie had ridden away—he had saddled Storm himself, and they'd managed to leave between guard changes—she had been terrified that spies loyal to the queen might discover the plan and arrest them. It seemed like she'd held her breath for hours, until the sound of horse hooves on gravel sent her into a half swoon against the wall…thoroughly unnerving for a woman who prided herself on her confidence in, and command of, all situations.

Now the terror had abated somewhat to be replaced by emotions equally as poisonous to well-being: jealousy and despair.

Now that Lachlan and Marjorie were wed, they were lost to her, for they wouldn't need a mistress at all. They would leave and set up their own household, bed only each other, maybe remember her fondly for a time with brief letters that would dwindle to nothing as the months passed. Eventually, she might look upon this act with a quiet pride and contentment that she had put others above herself and also thwarted that damned child-queen. But not now. This moment, agonizing pain clawed her insides, the kind she'd never wanted to experience again: the pain of loss. Doubly worse, for not just one snatched from her but two. Already she knew that never again would there be another Lachlan and Marjorie, eagerly submissive lovers who suited her so well. Never again would the solar bear witness to the glorious passion only found in three. And this knowledge was *crushing*.

A knock at the door sounded, and Janet turned and glared at the oak. "I asked…I asked not to be disturbed," she managed from a boulder-clogged throat.

"It is Marjorie and Lachlan, mistress."

Janet stilled at the muffled feminine reply, her heart lurching. She did not believe for a moment they had bedded each other already. And Marjorie had said *mistress*.

Setting down her goblet on a side table, Janet walked

over to the chamber door and opened it slowly. "Come in."

The two entered the room like penitent students, heads bowed and hands at their sides. Further stunned and more than a little intrigued, Janet folded her arms and tilted her head. "It is done?"

"Partly," said Lachlan, dropping to one knee before reaching into his doublet and pulling out two small, tightly rolled scrolls, each with a red wax seal affixed.

"Partly?" she repeated, taking one of the scrolls and locking it within a cleverly hidden compartment in the large wooden chest at the foot of her bed. Lachlan could keep the other copy in his own chamber; it was never sensible to keep two in the same place. Especially with documents as important as these—apart from Master Shaw, the papers were all they had to prove that a formal promise of marriage had taken place.

"Wedded...but not bedded, mistress," said Marjorie. "We...we decided it felt wrong without you."

Tears burned her eyes, forcing Janet to take a deep breath for composure. "Did you now?" she replied softly, turning back to look at them both.

"Aye," said Lachlan, his dark gaze both hot and yielding in a way that made her squeeze her thighs together against a rush of pure arousal.

"Well then. I can see you are both dusty from your ride to town. Best you undress and have a sponge bath before such an important occasion as a marital bedding."

As Lachlan began to remove his doublet, Janet crossed the chamber to latch the door. When she returned, she assisted Marjorie with her hood, leaf-green gown, kirtle, and shift. Soon the newlyweds stood naked—Lachlan unperturbed, Marjorie clearly at war with herself as she resisted the urge to cover her breasts and mound as taught her whole life.

Both belonged to Janet Fraser.

Excitement entwined with pure relief surged, and when Janet dipped a sponge into a bowl of cool water sprinkled with herbs that rested on a stand, her hand trembled and made a small splash.

She went to Marjorie first, gently sponging her back, bottom, and legs. Then she moved to stand in front of her ward before attending to her neck, arms, and stomach. Naturally, she took special care with those delectable plump breasts, rubbing the damp and slightly rough sponge over Marjorie's swollen nipples until the younger woman quivered. After rewetting the sponge, Janet trailed it down between Marjorie's thighs, parting the brown bush of hair and dragging it back and forth against the petal-soft pink flesh, smiling when Marjorie whimpered with need but deliberately denying her release.

"Now you, pet," she purred, wetting the sponge once again.

Lachlan shuddered, and without prompting, placed his hands atop his head. Already his magnificent cock had grown thicker and longer, and her mouth watered to suck it down her throat. But no. Her Beast would have to wait for such pleasures. Instead, she tormented him with the sponge, firmer than she'd been with Marjorie, although she lightened her touch when washing his scars. The naughty man had removed the bandage she'd applied at the loch, but his most recent wound appeared to be healing well. Last of all she washed his cock, dropping the sponge and instead using her hands to roughly massage the engorged length until he pleaded to be permitted to spend. But she denied him release too.

"What next?" said Marjorie, her eyes wide and cheeks flushed, the heady scent of her wet cunt perfuming the chamber.

"You'll both pleasure me first," said Janet. "Marjorie,

help me with my gown. Lachlan, fetch the brown bottle of oil from my satchel."

Minutes later she stood as naked as her lovers. Both poured a small quantity of oil into their palms and began to rub it into her skin; Marjorie attending to her front and Lachlan her back.

Janet barely stifled a moan as Marjorie's soft fingers tweaked her nipples, a delicious contrast to Lachlan's strong hands on her back, rubbing the knots of tension from her shoulders. When her needy cunt couldn't bear any more luscious teasing, she twisted to take each hand and guide them down between her legs.

"Duel," Janet commanded harshly.

"I…um…what?" asked Marjorie, biting her lip.

Lachlan pressed closer. "Ease your fingers…in the m-mistress's cunt. I'll ease mine…in her arse. A duel 'til release."

Marjorie brightened. "Oh! I see. I may lack experience, but I warn you, husband, I shall win this battle."

"Not a chance," rasped Lachlan, his oiled fingers circling Janet's back entrance.

At the gentle press of two fingers into her cunt and two fingers into her back entrance, Janet gasped in delight. But when they began a wondrous duel of thrusts and strokes only separated by thin flesh, a wild cry burst from her lips. Lachlan wrapped his free arm about her waist to hold her up, yet his marauding fingers were relentless, as were Marjorie's. Then he bit her neck just as Marjorie laved her right nipple, and Janet barely muffled her scream of ecstasy as a violent, prolonged release tore through her trembling body.

Sheer perfection.

When Janet at last regained her senses, she gently dislodged both, then walked over to her bed. When she'd arranged herself on the pillows, a wicked smile lifted her lips.

Now they would receive their reward: a marital bedding like no other.

"Do join me, newlyweds."

• • •

She was a wedded wife. And soon, so soon, she would be a bedded one.

Quivering with a combination of excitement, anticipation, and anxiety about the unknown, Marjorie allowed Lachlan to escort her over to the bed.

What an overwhelming day of twists and turns it had been: The lighthearted fun and gentle intimacy of their time beside the stream. That terrible letter from the queen that had turned her world upside down. Janet's knowledge and Lachlan's comfort to devise a plan. A hasty, irregular, and possibly treasonous marriage in a lawyer's chambers. And now, the occasion she'd awaited so long…learning all the secrets of the marriage bed. If she'd had to do this with an elderly English stranger, it would have been unbearable. But she had Lachlan—her gruff, brawny hero—and Janet, her lusty and commanding mistress, and although the unknown and the possibility of pain were unnerving, she was eager to begin and share this special moment with them.

Together, she and Lachlan had willingly served their mistress and brought her to a screaming release with their wicked duel. Now it was their turn to pleasure each other as Janet instructed.

"Come sit here, between my legs, Marjorie dear," said Janet as she lounged on the pillows, her thighs spread wide, one hand lazily stroking her jutting nipples.

Taking a deep breath, Marjorie climbed onto the large bed and crawled into position, settling herself against Janet's breasts. Her mistress clearly understood the emotions swirling within her, for she began to stroke her skin and murmur words of encouragement before kissing her on the mouth, light kisses that soon turned deeply passionate.

She moaned, drawing away to catch her breath. "I don't...I don't know what to do. How it is supposed to be."

"How do you w-wish it to be?" asked Lachlan, perched on the side of the bed.

Marjorie smiled at his care and courtesy. His cock was so hard and ready for release he was clearly in discomfort, but not by so much as a twitch had he insisted upon his need being met before hers. "I should like, ah, to be touched some more before you, er, enter me. If you are willing."

"Oh, my dear," said Janet, very seriously. "We shall both ensure you are ready. I know the first time can be overwhelming because you just don't know. It can be a little unpleasant to start as your body adjusts; occasionally there is pain and some bleeding. But while it is our duty to assist and support and pleasure you, it is your duty to tell us how you are feeling, whether something is not enough or just right or too much, because we cannot know your mind. Do you understand?"

"Yes, mistress," said Marjorie huskily as a slow throb began between her legs. Janet explained lusty matters so clearly. It was so freeing, so reassuring, to know exactly what she must do rather than awkwardly stumble, and that she might stop something she did not enjoy. "Kiss me, Lachlan."

He leaned over and cupped her cheek before brushing his lips against hers. But she did not want such gentleness, instead curving a hand around his neck and kissing him back firmly, her tongue darting against his lips until he opened his mouth and kissed her properly.

Janet really was a most excellent tutor.

"What next?" rasped Lachlan eventually, his chest rising and falling, and it did her heart good to know he was equally affected by their kisses.

"I want…I want…please, Janet, touch my breasts. And Lachlan…down there."

He hesitated and glanced at Janet.

"No, dear one," said her stern mistress. "*Down there* is not sufficient. If you wish him to kiss your pearl, say so. If you wish him to stroke or lick your sweet little cunt, say so. He will do as you desire, but you must state plainly what that desire is. Do not force us to withhold release from you in punishment."

Marjorie squirmed on the bed at the reprimand. She had indeed been instructed many times on plain speaking and did indeed know better. Now was not the time to retreat to the comfortable familiarity of convent virgin. She was a married woman with a husband and a mistress, who had been well taught on how to give and receive pleasure.

"It aches, Lachlan," she whispered. "My…my *cunt* aches. Use your tongue until I scream. Until I make your mouth all wet."

"There now," said Janet, and Marjorie whimpered when those nimble fingers rewarded her candor with caresses and light pinches of her swollen nipples.

Lachlan moved to kneel between her spread legs. By the saints, the way he was looking at her right now, reverent and yet so hungry, as he ran his hands along her sturdy thighs, as he carefully parted the crisp brown hair that covered her mound and exposed her silky-wet and spicy-scented pink flesh. She felt beautiful. Desirable. And that was lovely indeed.

Janet laughed. "Cunt-struck, pet?"

"Aye. Only one other…so perfect."

"Then *feast*."

At the first flick of her husband's tongue across her aching pearl, such a jolt of sensation raced through Marjorie's body that she jerked and moaned. But with his huge hands resting on her thighs, and Janet cupping her breasts and kissing her neck, she was a willing captive. Then he dragged his tongue again and again from her pearl to her back entrance, pausing only to push his tongue inside her and coat it with the honey trickling from her center. With each movement his short beard rasped her inner thighs, and the contrast of gentle and rough was so delicious she couldn't help the bucking of her hips in an attempt to get closer or the choked cries escaping her lips. A little more…just a little more…

All at once he pressed hard on her pearl with his thumb and drove his tongue deep inside her, hurling her over the edge into a storm of bliss. Fortunately Janet had the foresight to muffle her scream of pleasure with a firm hand; otherwise every servant in the manor would have come running.

Lachlan inhaled shakily and licked his lips. "Again."

Even in the foggy mist of pleasure aftermath, that seemed wrong. She was soaking wet, had been carefully prepared for his cock, was ready and eager to feel him inside her…and he did not enter her? It was plainly obvious he wanted to. His manhood bobbed against his abdomen, hard and thick, a little pearly seed dampening the tip. She could see the need in his eyes, the strain at holding back.

Perplexed, she reached out and placed a hand on his shoulder. "Why are you denying me your cock? Why are you denying yourself?"

Color darkened his cheeks. "You aren't quite ready."

Marjorie frowned. "Beg pardon?" she replied, affronted. She most certainly was ready!

Janet cleared her throat. "I know you mean well, pet, but that is for your wife, not you, to decide. Besides, a cunt is most robust. It is made to stretch. Now, do get on with your husbandly duty."

He glanced at Marjorie, his expression rueful. "Forgive me."

She grinned mischievously. "Only if you *fuck* me. Is that plain enough?"

Lachlan did smile then, his eyes glinting with amusement. "Aye, lady wife. Most plain."

Moments later he took his length in hand and rubbed the head against her slick center. Then, he began to penetrate her.

Marjorie gasped at the stretch, the overwhelming feeling of fullness, and winced at the brief stinging pain as he eased his cock in. But when he settled into an easy rhythm of advance and retreat, pushing his cock in before slowly easing out, it felt better, then much better, then very, very good. Deciding then and there that Lachlan moved with entirely too much caution, she dug her heels into the bed and thrust upward, embedding him fully inside her.

A guttural groan tore from his throat as he thrust harder. "So hot…so tight…so good…"

"More," said Marjorie greedily, her nails scratching his back, her legs locking tightly around his waist to hold him to her, desperate to reach the blissful release that teased her once again.

"Spend," Janet commanded harshly.

She cried out as her inner walls clamped around Lachlan's cock, and a wave of sensation sent her soaring to the stars, only made better by the sound of her husband's low roar of ecstasy, the gush of his seed flooding deep inside her.

Indeed, a wedding bedding to remember.

Chapter Ten

The air was heavy with the scent of ecstasy, the sounds of gasping breaths and twitching bodies sliding across crisp linen sheets.

Janet smiled as Lachlan and Marjorie settled themselves on either side of her, glad they had the foresight to move so she wasn't crushed beneath their combined weight. Her chamber—or more specifically, her bed—had become a sanctuary for forbidden lust, and although she well knew that sanctuary was an illusion…for the moment she would embrace the feeling of peace. Of gratitude that the bedding had gone so well, that she had been a part of it. Well, more than that. She had been in *command* of it.

"How are you both?" asked Janet. "After that important task."

Marjorie cuddled closer, tucking her head into Janet's shoulder even as she reached across and clasped Lachlan's hand. "I am well. I couldn't have hoped for a better first time. With you both. I feel…so fortunate. I mean…it hurt a little bit at first. Like a pinch. Then it didn't. Lachlan moving helped the ache, but he moved too slow. So I...ah...helped him along."

Janet couldn't help but laugh. "You are impatient, dear one."

"I know. 'Tis my flaw. Lachlan, I hope I didn't hurt you with my fingernails."

He looked briefly startled. "No. Not at all."

"And you, Lachlan? Now you are a wedded and bedded husband?" said Janet.

He hesitated. "It was wonderful. But..."

"But?" said Marjorie, tensing. "What is the matter?"

Lachlan sighed and propped himself up on one elbow. "I must beg forgiveness. I did n-not ask your w-wishes. In spending, I mean. Outside or in."

"I don't understand. Why would you spend outside? You must do so in, so I might conceive a child. I would like a baby more than anything. Son or daughter, I do not mind. I have always wanted to be a mother, ever since I was a little girl, and now that I have a husband, it is right and proper to do so."

Janet closed her eyes, trying not to flinch as each innocent arrow found its mark and ripped open a wound that refused to heal. Of course Marjorie and Lachlan should have a conversation about children. She had encouraged them to speak plainly of their desires and needs. But so soon, and in bed? She was ill prepared, without the armor of clothing or distance or an activity to distract. Here with two people she cared deeply for, she might not be able to mask the pain of her barrenness. She had felt wretched earlier thinking them snatched from her, then bedding in private...but this was far too much. Poor Marjorie did not know the agony she caused. She would probably be mortified. And it wasn't her fault; a new wife longing for motherhood would naturally be excited for the future.

But devil take it, the hurt did not lessen. Time did not

heal or bring acceptance.

She had been confused but a little relieved as the months passed and her belly did not swell with the king's child, as his attentions were enjoyable and she hadn't felt ready to be a mother. But when the months turned into years, the confusion had turned into fear. She'd been advised to take tonics, to bed in certain positions, to pray. Nothing. Others had insisted it would be different in the holy bonds of matrimony, yet her belly remained flat with Fergus also.

Her husband had been so calm, so understanding, each month when she bled. She had raged and wept, pleaded and threatened and cajoled. It made no difference. Each month, as night followed day, her body taunted her with the harsh reminder there was something she could not command. And no manuscript, no ancient wisdom or physician, could explain why. Even her own knowledge of herbals…worthless. Worst of all, she was constantly surrounded by women succeeding. Shared tales of early nausea and fatigue, swollen bellies and ankles, the triumph of a healthy birth. All of James's other mistresses had given him a child; before he'd wed Margaret Tudor, the cherished bairns had resided at Stirling Castle.

But Janet had failed.

And every time there came a new pregnancy or birth announcement, she had to be delighted. Smile even as her broken heart shattered once more and buried her under a rockslide of *why*. Why must she be the barren one? Why must she suffer the annoyance of bleeding and belly gripes each month but never the jolt of a little kick or the tranquility of rocking an infant to sleep? Not once had Fergus scolded or blamed her, nor had he yelled or hurled a single item. After a while they'd stopped speaking of children at all, and she'd been torn whether to love him more for such kindness or hate his admittance of defeat.

To be bested by strength, wit, or learning was one thing.

Bested by your own body?

Soul destroying.

"Janet?" said Marjorie, her brow furrowing. "Are you well?"

No!

She gritted her teeth. "Of course. I just need to use the chamber pot. Do let me out, my dear, or I shall be worse than an untrained pup."

Marjorie grinned and shuffled toward the pillows to give her room. "Yes, mistress."

As sweet freedom from the emotional tempest beckoned, Janet sat up and prepared to flee. Until Lachlan put his hand on her arm.

"Are you sure…you are w-well? Not upset?"

A pox on the man for knowing her history. Why did he have to *see*?

"Quite well, pet," said Janet, twisting away from him and swinging her legs over the side of the bed. "Also quite serious about my need to use the chamber pot."

Hurrying over to the other side of the room and behind an embroidered screen she could kiss right now for the privacy it provided, Janet covered her mouth and shrieked into her hand. Yes, it changed nothing. But if she did not lance the wound, it would fester inside her, and she did not have the luxury of tears. Although, later she would be drinking enough wine to launch a ship at supper.

Lachlan clearing his throat sounded like thunder rumbling in the silence. "Do you think, mistress…Marjorie conceiving a c-child would help…or hinder us?"

Janet shrieked into her hand again, furious when a tiny squeak escaped. Then she took several breaths, squared her shoulders, and walked back around the screen as though her burdens were feather light rather than crushing boulders.

"I cannot be certain, of course. However, it seems rational

that the king and clergy might be less inclined to protest a union that would leave an innocent babe a bastard. If you are both ready to welcome a child early in your marriage, then by all means try for one...we really must dress. I'm sure suppertime is fast approaching, and we must not give any of the servants cause for concern."

Lachlan looked like he might say something further, but she held up a hand and added a stern glare for good measure, and he fell silent.

No. She would permit no more distressing talk until she'd drained the manor dry of wine. Or celebrated her hundredth birthday.

Preferably the latter.

• • •

Lady Janet was not well. Not at all.

Lachlan pressed his lips together so he did not speak as he swiftly sponged himself with the cool cloth by the bowl of water, then dressed.

His mistress wore the same brittle, unhappy expression she had at the supper with the Campbells and the Sinclairs and the thoughtless comment about a woman's true purpose. He knew her past miseries; the king had often spoken of Lady Janet's sadness, his own disappointment in not having a child with his fiery one. Today he had been equally as thoughtless as Jean Sinclair, blurting out those words in front of Lady Janet when he could have easily spoken to Marjorie privately.

Damned fool.

The marital bedding had gone so well with the three of them together, as he was starting to believe they should be forever. Lusty and pleasurable and powerful. Then he had ruined it— twice, in fact. First the spending discussion, then asking Lady Janet's opinion on a possible pregnancy for

Marjorie.

Baseborn, hell-spawned fool.

Grimly, he watched Lady Janet and Marjorie help each other with their shifts, kirtles, and gowns. His wife kept biting her lip and glancing at their mistress, a sure sign she was troubled but didn't know what to say. Not that he knew either. Even if he did, no doubt it would tumble out all wrong. Lady Janet had been so generous, so accepting of his speech affliction. Yet she shied away like an unbroken colt when it came to matters concerning herself, especially something that might disturb her sense of control and command. If she did not wish to discuss her barrenness, he had to respect her wishes, even if the stone wall and moat she had built around her heart hurt him.

"I wonder what we are having for supper," said Marjorie awkwardly into the silence. "I find I am hungry. Very hungry."

Lady Janet smiled briefly as she smoothed her hair and adjusted her hood. "It has been quite the day. I understand there will be beef. Fowl also. I must admit, after living at Stirling Castle—and before that, traveling with the king and his privy councillors—I forgot how many tasks are involved in running a household. Food and supplies, linens, stables, servants' wages and other expenses…attending to the finer details is not something I enjoy overmuch. I prefer to lead the army—or at least entertain them rather than decide how many carrots they may eat or which color hose they wear."

"I wonder if," said Marjorie very, very tentatively, "I could help?"

Lachlan almost laughed at the thought of a lady eager to take on those menial tasks, until he saw the wistfulness on her face. "At the convent," he asked, "did you have…such duties?"

She twisted her fingers together. "The only nun who didn't tell me to run along and stop bothering her was Sister

Elspeth in the kitchens. Her mind was sharp, but her eyes and hands were not so well anymore. So I helped her make lists. What we grew in the gardens, the supply of butter and herbs, of grain and flour. Each week I would make note of all our supplies and tell her. Then when the men came from town in their wagons, with fish and fowl or other goods, I helped to purchase them. Sister Elspeth showed me how to select the best. To know when I was being cheated. Some of the men thought a nun would be sweet and kind and would forgive them their sins if they did so, but Sister Elspeth set the kitchen dog onto them. He was mean and liked to bite ankles and bottoms. They soon learned to bring only the best."

This time Lachlan couldn't halt the laugh that rumbled in his chest. Even the thought of sweet little Marjorie and a wily old nun placidly watching a feral kitchen dog latch onto a merchant's arse after he tried to cheat them with less-than-fresh food...

"Lady Janet," he said gruffly. "Maybe you could...train Marjorie in your p-preferences. Allow her to assist you. Ease your b-burden."

Marjorie beamed at him before turning to Lady Janet with so much hope in her eyes it was almost painful to witness. "May I? I should so like to be useful to you. All your favorite foods and wines, and only the freshest and best goods from town. I would personally ensure your table is the finest in St. Andrews. Oh yes, and that you always have the herbs you need for your tonics and poultices."

Lady Janet held up both hands. "Very well. Very well! I cede control of the larder. You can take charge of the linen cupboard also. Mind you don't become a tyrant, though. Save that for the marketplace when some fool tries to sell you fish so old it has gray hairs sprouting from the gills. Now, let us go downstairs to supper before they send an army to find us."

Marjorie near twirled toward the chamber door, but

Lachlan paused and stared hard at Lady Janet. "Mistress—"

"No, pet," she replied softly but firmly. "I have been flung in several directions today, and all I want this night is a full belly and an empty goblet. To make merry. One thing I am equally certain about is a strong aversion to prying questions regarding the private body matter that half of Scotland knows about because everyone shares and comments on it."

Lachlan hesitated, then took her hand and squeezed it. "Just know…we are here. That we care. If you ever wish to t-talk. As we did b-by the stream."

Lady Janet's face shuttered. "I am glad that discussion bought you comfort, but I do not wish the same for my matter. I've had enough advice, enough suspicious looks, and enough blunt questions to last ten lifetimes. I *will not* be pitied. If you cannot obey that simple command…"

Although her voice trailed off, Lachlan knew what she meant, and icy cold fear slithered down his spine. To be banished from Lady Janet's presence, to live in a world without the fire that warmed him, that urged him to be better…to be without the woman who understood his desire to be owned and commanded in the bedchamber, and brought him greater pleasure than he'd ever known…

Unthinkable.

"As you wish, lady," he conceded, willing to say anything to return to her good graces, to make her forget that he'd been a blundering fool. As a bastard son, he well knew how it felt to be the object of talk, and as someone who'd had difficulty speaking for as long as he could remember, he also knew how tiresome and sometimes infuriating the advice and pity could be.

No one wanted to be noted for an affliction, one thing they could not change. Especially when they worked so very hard to succeed in other aspects of their lives. He had honed weaponry and battle to a fine art, and Lady Janet was a bold, learned, lusty woman who had conquered kings, nobles, and common men alike.

To have her affection, to live in this manor and sleep in her bed, was a miracle for a man who had long ago stopped believing in such things.

Nothing could be allowed to spoil that.

Nothing.

...

She had done something terribly wrong but had no idea what it was.

Marjorie gripped her wine goblet tighter as dismay churned around and around in her stomach. Supper had indeed been beef and fowl, roasted, with several sauces, plus a selection of jellies, puddings, vegetables, and poached pears in cream. She had eaten more than her fill due to the stilted conversation at the table and Janet's coolness, and now her belly might well burst open.

Her very first proper bedding had been wonderful. More than wonderful—pure bliss. Never had she felt so free to be herself, so cared for, in her entire life. And then it had all gone wrong. Somehow, she had angered or displeased Janet, one of the two people she would never, ever wish to hurt, and that knowledge clawed her heart.

What on earth could it be?

Marjorie watched in miserable silence as servants bustled about, clearing away the platters of uneaten food, which they would soon enjoy for their own supper. If Janet was particularly angry, would she change her mind in allowing her ward to oversee aspects of the household? That would be a terrible blow. Being alone and unwanted at the convent, then Stirling Castle, had been punishment enough. To be unwanted here...she might not recover from that.

Abruptly, Janet pushed her chair back and got to her feet. "Forgive me, both of you, but I think I shall retire for the evening. I can scarcely keep my eyes open."

Lachlan pressed his hands to the table. "Should we—"

"No."

The word was said gently but had the impact of a boulder crashing through a roof.

Stricken, Marjorie rose to her feet so quickly her chair tumbled backward with a clatter onto the hall floor. "Janet, what is the matter? What is wrong?"

"Do not fret. I am just very tired. I shall see you in the morning, and we'll talk further on your duties in regard to the larder and linen closet. Good night, Lachlan. Do escort Marjorie to her chamber when she is ready."

In stunned silence, they watched their mistress depart the hall without a backward glance. Yet Janet hadn't marched away at her usual brisk pace, or even walked. It had been more of a shuffle, her shoulders stooped, as though she carried the weight of several castles. As though she had been *defeated*.

And somehow, that was worse than anything else.

What could possibly defeat a bold tempest like Janet Fraser?

"Lachlan," she said hoarsely. "What just happened? I feel like I have done or said something terrible, but I don't know what it is, and I cannot bear it."

He hesitated, taking far too much care in removing the linen napkin draped over his left shoulder and placing it on the table, and perspiration broke out on her neck. Lachlan knew what it was but did not know how to say it.

By the saints, it truly must be something awful.

"Tell me," Marjorie demanded, yanking off her own napkin and hurling it onto the table. "Tell me or I shall go mad."

"Let's go upstairs," he replied, failing utterly in his

attempt at a reassuring smile.

After setting her chair to rights and nodding their thanks to the servants clearing away the plates and goblets, Marjorie and Lachlan left the hall and made their way to her chamber. As soon as they were safely inside, away from curious eyes and ears, she hurried over to the fireplace. It wasn't a cold evening at all, but holding her hands in front of the healthy blaze and listening to the crackle and hiss of burning wood offered some blessed distraction.

"Tell me," she said, quietly this time.

Lachlan sighed and rubbed a hand across his face. "You weren't to know. H-how could you? And it is my f-fault, in truth. I said something thoughtless. You answered…as a new wife w-would. But we both hurt our mistress."

"*How?* What did I say?"

"When you spoke of…conceiving a child. Lady Janet is…b-barren, you see."

All the air fled her lungs, and Marjorie choked on a horrified gasp. "Oh no. That is…oh no. Lachlan, I was cruel! I didn't mean to be…but I was!"

Tears gathered in her eyes and began to spill down her cheeks. Even when his arm closed around her shoulders and pressed her to his chest, she couldn't entirely stop them, and she spent several moments sniffling and coughing in a most humiliating manner.

How could I not have known?

Yes, no one had told her, but the evidence was plain. Janet had been the virile king's mistress for a long time, and while he had several children to other women, they had none together. Then Janet had wed Master Fraser. And she'd had many other lovers, including Lachlan.

But no children. Never any children.

"I am a fool," Marjorie said painfully. "A fool who does not see what is right in front of her."

"*Not* a fool," said Lachlan as he patted her back. "Just unaware. But now you know. Also know this: Lady Janet d-does not wish…to speak of it. Ever. I believe it c-causes her…great pain."

She winced. "I understand. But what of us?"

Lachlan guided her to the chair in front of the fireplace before lowering himself to sit on the thick woven rug. "I have thirty summers. My life was…fighting for the k-king. I did not think of ch-children. My mother was wonderful. A strong woman. My father…uh…they did not wed."

"That is not your sin!"

"Yes. But I lived w-with it. I did not w-want a child t-to suffer as I d-did. Forgive me. My speech gets worse."

"There is nothing to forgive," she said firmly. "Please do go on if you can. I feel I need to know this, even if it stings."

Lachlan took a deep breath and curled his arms around his knees as though armoring himself. "I didn't think… to wed. No land, no home. A bastard knight. So I did not w-want children. But now I am w-wed."

Somehow, she forced the words out, both desperate to know and afraid to hear the answer. "So do you wish to have a child now? A child with me?"

He met her gaze unflinchingly, his face grave. "I am… unsure. Not because of you. But…"

Marjorie closed her eyes briefly, heartsick to her core. "Janet."

"And our marriage. The queen will f-find out. When you d-don't go to Carlisle. They may forgive. Or…they may not. I would n-not want to leave a f-fatherless infant. If I am…in prison."

Slumping back in the chair, Marjorie fought the urge to howl. Not a single thing Lachlan had said could be judged unfair or unreasonable. Their marriage was precarious at best, and one or both could indeed be punished severely for defying a royal decree. Not to mention, her conceiving a child would be very difficult for Janet.

And yet a small, selfish part of her wanted to scream: *What about me?*

In this fine chamber, when it might seem to an outsider that she had everything she wanted—a strong, protective husband; elegant home; friendship—she could feel her most cherished dream of being a mother slipping from her grasp.

Of all the heartbreaks and disappointments she had taken in her life, this might well be the hardest to bear.

Chapter Eleven

After several nights tossing and turning in his cold and lonely bed, his nickname of Beast had never felt more apt.

Lachlan scowled at the pile of old linen and straw at his feet. A half hour ago, they had been stuffed figures to train with in the small fenced area next to the stables, but not even imagining they were English and slicing them to shreds had improved his temper. Nor had his efforts before that: firing two dozen arrows at a target, hacking fallen tree branches for firewood, or assisting the head gardener till soil.

He might be fragrant with sweat, his muscles burning and twitching with fatigue, but nothing could quell his uncertainty or dread at the unspoken hurt, the cool politeness in the manor. And it wasn't due to his secret marriage; his conscience felt no pricks about that. But at the prospect of losing Lady Janet or Marjorie…his stomach churned relentlessly.

He had spoken thoughtlessly to Lady Janet that night of the bedding and hadn't been much better with Marjorie after that. The more he considered the thought of a child with his wife, the more the idea appealed. Just not yet. That is what he should have said; he would like to try for a child, but until they had a clear path for the future, the time wasn't quite right. Instead, he'd made it seem like Marjorie's wishes didn't matter at all.

Not only a failure as a lover but also a husband.

Damned fool.

Leaning down, he scooped up an armful of straw and dropped it into an old sack. The horses could stomp on the remains later in their stalls. Straw men certainly weren't the best for training—he did miss the king's armory and James himself to cross swords with—but he needed to remain ready and skilled to face any danger, and the guards here were busy in their duties. As each day took them closer to the queen's order of an escort for Marjorie to Carlisle, he watched the estate gates like a hawk, ready and willing to protect his ladies.

Swift steps on the cobblestoned courtyard made him tense and turn, but it was Lady Janet walking toward him.

"After such an active morning, you look like a knight in need of refreshment," she said, holding up a small flagon. "Ale?"

Lachlan nodded cautiously. "Aye."

"Consider it a peace offering, pet. I have not at all practiced what I preach, and that is to speak plainly. I have allowed distance to grow between us, which is the last thing I desire."

He took a long swallow of the ale, welcoming the liquid splash to his parched throat as much as the opportunity to gather his thoughts. But there was only one: a relief so great he almost staggered. "I have missed you. I have m-missed… the three of us."

Lady Janet flinched. "I have also. I hope we can set aside the matter of a child for a time and regain the happiness we found in each other."

"For a time," Lachlan agreed. "But we must t-talk of

it, mistress. Your w-wishes are important. Marjorie's are as well. B-both of you are hurting. I have been thoughtless. It is…a bramble p-patch."

"That it is. For today, at least, I would like the three of us to leave the manor for a little while. To attend the St. Andrews market. Marjorie could show us her skill in managing tradesman and merchants."

"Aye. I should change m-my shirt first. I must have…a scent about m-me."

A smile broke out on Lady Janet's face. "You do, pet. Eau de stable. And you have stray bits of straw in your hair. Attend to yourself, then meet us outside the stables in a quarter hour."

Once he'd changed into a fresh linen shirt, his usual red doublet, black hose, and mantle, Lachlan finger-combed his hair to ensure no rogue straw remained before returning to the courtyard. One of the stable lads was assisting Lady Janet onto her horse, and he took a moment to appreciate how fine she looked in her dark-green gown. Marjorie already sat atop her horse, equally lovely in blue, although she appeared uneasy as she glanced between mount and hard ground.

"Ladies," he said, tipping his hat.

Lady Janet raised an eyebrow. "Courtly of you."

"Impressed?"

"Not overly. Leap a moat or ride up a staircase on that mighty steed of yours, all blindfolded, however…"

"I shall k-keep that in mind. Marjorie, how might…I impress you?"

His wife tapped her chin. "Fetch me a handful of stars and a unicorn to ride."

Lachlan smiled as he settled onto Storm's saddle. The three of them did indeed have much to speak on, but already the air seemed lighter, and his spirits rose. He loved Lady Janet, and his affection for Marjorie grew stronger every day. The two ladies cared a great deal for each other also. Surely nothing could truly come between them.

The guards knew of their planned jaunt to town and respectfully waved them through the main gate. Unlike last time, when he and Marjorie had ridden like the wind to St. Andrews, today's journey was a comfortable trot. While the breeze was crisp and made him glad of his fur-lined mantle, the sun was trying to peek through clouds and warm them.

"Is it a very large market here?" asked Marjorie.

"Haven't been for years," he admitted. "But they are held w-weekly. On Market Street. Most people attend. You might see…some Blackfriars. And Grayfriars."

"Blackfriars are Dominican order, Grayfriars are Franciscan," explained Lady Janet.

"Oh!" said Marjorie. "I see. At the convent, merchants and tradesmen had wagons of goods or stalls they used to set up just outside the walls. Do they do the same here?"

Lachlan nodded. "If they have coin. Others lay wares on c-cloaks or blankets."

His wife wriggled on her saddle, her excitement clear. "I cannot wait to admire everything. Well, admire all that is fresh and well made, of course. Anything else shall feel the full weight of my scorn and wrath."

Lady Janet laughed. "And that is what I cannot wait to admire."

The manor was only a few miles from the town proper, and in little time a sprinkling of crofter cottages—with their small plots of land boasting rows of vegetables, pig pens, and hen houses—came into view. Approaching from the south as they were, soon they would be able to see the upper reaches of St. Andrews castle to the left and the cathedral to the right, two ancient and imposing stone guardians that had stood between the town and sea for hundreds of years.

Yet Lachlan shifted uncomfortably in his saddle. It might be because the town was one of the holiest places in Scotland

and because of his own uneasy relationship with God, but he felt on edge that no word had arrived from Stirling about Marjorie's proposed marriage or details on travel arrangements. It made him suspicious. His late mother had taught him as a young lad to never ignore his instincts, and that advice had served him well, even saved his life on a few occasions.

Glancing left and right, he watched townspeople go about their day. They seemed innocent enough, but as he well knew, people were not always as they seemed.

In this market town full of strangers, he would need to keep his wits about him.

...

Last time she had set foot in St. Andrews, she had been too anxious, too overwhelmed, too rushed in her haste to be wed to really notice anything about the town.

This time, she could admire *everything.*

Marjorie gripped her reins, lest she slide from her saddle as her head jerked up and down and left and right, trying to see all that was around her as they reached the bottom of Market Street. Tradesmen and merchants had set up stalls the entire length of it, and even from here she could see trays of vegetables; pens containing chickens, pigs, and cows; tinkers selling pots, pans, and knives; a stall entirely of leather goods; many selling various fabrics; even a smithy working metal and a carpenter sanding a small table while onlookers watched. There were several fishmongers bellowing about fresh catch, and her nose wrinkled at the briny scent combined with tilled soil, meat roasting on spits, and small piles of manure.

"Fragrant, isn't it?"

She turned to Janet, who regarded her with glinting eyes. To have her mistress look at her with fondness again rather than distant politeness relieved her no end. The last few days in the manor had stretched her nerves to breaking point, but as Janet refused to discuss how her barrenness hurt her, or the matter of a child, how to proceed had been unclear.

Saints willing, today could change everything.

"So fragrant," Marjorie agreed. "I just hope when I dismount, I land in cool dirt rather than something fresh and warm."

"Indeed. We should probably tie up the horses at this end of the street rather than further down. The closer we get to the cathedral, the busier it will be. So many pilgrims travel here, wanting to look at the relics."

"*Relics*," Lachlan grunted, sliding from his mount before handing the reins and a coin to one of the young lads offering to feed, water, and walk horses in a roped-off square. "So they say."

After he helped them both from their horses, Marjorie tentatively approached her guardian. To her delight, Janet linked arms with her, and they began to walk.

"I must beg forgiveness," she blurted. "I did not know about your, ah…"

"Barrenness?"

"I feel so terrible. Chattering on and on and all the while causing you pain—"

"No, dear one," said Janet, shaking her head. "Not here. I swear we shall speak of the matter soon and come to some agreement where we can *all* be happy. For now…think about what you shall beg me for when we return to the manor, retreat to the solar, and make use of that sturdy chaise."

Marjorie quivered. Touching herself had brought some relief the past few endless nights alone in bed, but nothing in the world could compare to the soul-shattering pleasure she'd known with Janet and Lachlan. "I…I can think of a few things."

"So eager. You've missed your lessons, then?"

Janet's tone and smile were indulgent, but a hint of

something far deeper lurked in her eyes. Almost as though her bold, commanding mistress felt a little uncertain. And to that, she could only give honesty. Probably too much, too soon, but after so much upheaval, she did not want to hide her true feelings any longer. Who knew what the future would hold for them all?

"So much," said Marjorie rawly. "I need you, as I need Lachlan. In bed and out. Always. I...I love you."

Janet swallowed hard, her gaze softening, her hand tightening on Marjorie's arm. "Well. *Well*. That is sweet music to my ears. I...ah...where is your husband? Lachlan, stop scowling at the cathedral, or you'll be struck by lightning."

He joined them and grunted again. "*Relics*. Probably chicken bones. Or some unfortunate duck."

"Have you seen them?"

"Yes. Have you?"

Janet rolled her eyes. "One cannot be part of the king's retinue and not see them."

"What is it like?" Marjorie demanded, both disappointed Janet had avoided expressing herself fully once again and curious about the holy place she'd heard so much about. "Inside St. Andrews cathedral, I mean."

"Warm," said Lachlan, as he placed his hand at her back and rubbed it in that wonderfully soothing manner, just the way she enjoyed. "There are...so many candles. That and the incense...stings the eyes."

Janet nodded. "They do burn a lot of incense. But it is quite magnificent inside, dear one. You enter the north doors and progress to the relics. There are a great many shrines, and as Lachlan said, all lit up with candles. Also stained-glass windows, brightly painted effigies...St. Andrew at the highest point, of course...then you get to the casse, the jeweled box containing the bones. In truth I cannot be certain that they are real. But when you are there...it *feels* real. And it seems that is enough for the pilgrims. Now. We must look at these stalls so I can witness your best scorn and wrath."

Marjorie grinned reluctantly. "Which stall first?"

"Fishmonger?" said Lachlan, gesturing to a large stall several feet away. "We know how…you adore fish."

"Oh, you!" she replied, swatting her husband's chest when he puckered his lips and made a kissing sound, possibly the most playful act of his life. "*Beast.*"

"So they say."

Marjorie blushed at the warmth in his eyes. With Janet's wicked promise still echoing in her mind, and now Lachlan's palpable tenderness, she wanted to leave the market and return to the manor at once so they could reunite properly. After days without their touch, she craved them both more than air. "I…ah…"

"Devil take it."

Startled at the curse, she glanced at Janet, but her mistress's gaze was directed down Market Street, and her smile had vanished. "What do you see?"

"The Campbells are here. Hamish, Aileen, and that wretched peacock Angus."

Wishing the fashionable man to purgatory, Marjorie gritted her teeth. The incident in the garden had been unpleasant, but what the snake had done after that, she would never forgive him for. *He* was responsible for the queen deciding she must swiftly wed the English baron in Carlisle. *He* had nearly ruined her life with his petulant act of vengeance when she had rejected his advances. It might be due to Lachlan's warrior influence, but her thoughts at this moment were bloodthirsty rather than forgiving as she'd been taught. The prioress and nuns would be horrified, although Sister Elspeth and her kitchen dog might understand the sentiment.

In truth, the thought of that dog taking a large nip of Angus's bottom cheered her greatly.

"I won't speak to them," Marjorie announced, uncaring if the Campbells thought her impolite or cold, as her would-be lover had accused.

"He's fortunate…to retain all limbs," growled Lachlan.

Janet folded her arms. "I won't speak to Angus; that hell-spawned rodent is dead to me. But I should greet Hamish. And Aileen."

Marjorie stilled. Something in the way Janet said the other woman's name didn't ease her temper but made her want to spit needles. "How do you know her, really?"

"I told you at that supper," said Janet, looking away. "We shared a tutor a long time ago."

"Mistress," said Lachlan, frowning. "We deserve truth."

Her guardian's expression turned hunted, and Marjorie's heart plummeted. Indeed, there was certainly more to the tale than a shared tutor.

Janet straightened her shoulders. Then she sighed. "Yes, you do. Aileen…her father's lands marched alongside my father's. We saw each other often. We did share a tutor, but…"

"But?" whispered Marjorie, glancing across at Lachlan. He looked as grim as she felt.

"Aileen was my lover. My first. And a woman I once loved."

...

Devil take it, why did everything wonderful have to be swiftly followed by disaster?

Janet winced, an action becoming all too familiar. For a woman who prided herself on plain speaking, she tied herself in terrible knots when it came to her two lovers. And by the hurt on Marjorie's face and Lachlan's impassiveness, that mask he only wore when concealing a great deal of emotion, she had blundered badly. Again.

Marjorie had declared her love. And she'd been so overcome that she'd babbled like an infant and changed the subject. The worst possible subject. How foolish she'd been not to tell Marjorie and Lachlan the truth about Aileen after that supper. Naturally it had been prudent not to speak of it with blissfully unaware Hamish and Angus at the table, but she'd had ample opportunity to do so since then.

"I should have confessed," said Janet into the heavy silence. "It was wrong of me not to tell the whole tale."

"Why did you not tell us?" asked Marjorie, her beautiful face ashen.

"I'm not sure. I honestly did not know Aileen and Hamish lived near the manor, so it was a great shock to learn they were the supper guests. I have not seen either of them in many years. Since that summer, in fact. Aileen and I were discovered naked together, you see. My parents sent me to court as a gift to the king, and her parents arranged a hasty marriage."

"Do you still"—Lachlan pursed his lips as though he'd tasted something bitter—"care for her?"

At least this question she could answer.

Being alone with Aileen, she'd not felt any desire to retreat into the past. Not even a kiss or embrace. She would always remember that summer...more so for what she had learned of herself: that she lusted for women as well as men. Also some regret that their affair had been halted by others rather than coming to its own end as it should, so each could have walked away knowing they had not found their forever love and to keep searching. It had been that way with James. Yes, she had loved Fergus dearly and would always miss him, but she now knew for certain that her heart had found two new people to settle on: Lachlan and Marjorie.

Janet took a deep breath. "Let me explain it thus—"

"Lady Janet!"

At the booming hail from Hamish Campbell, she wanted to hurl manure at his chest, which was quite unfair. Unlike his rodent brother, Hamish remained an amiable, decent man. "Master Campbell," she said, then shifted her gaze. "Aileen."

Angus glared at her when she did not greet him but remarkably remained silent.

Aileen held out a hand, her smile forced. "Will you walk with me, Janet?"

A chill of unease slithered down her spine at the odd request. They really didn't have anything to discuss that required privacy. "Why?"

"Just over here for a bit," Aileen coaxed. "Come along, now."

Janet glanced back at her lovers. Marjorie shook her head, her eyes pleading and face even paler than before. Lachlan's hand moved to his sword hilt, his gaze menacing as it rested on the Campbells, but he, too, said nothing. "I'd rather not. I'm here with Sir Lachlan and Lady Marjorie."

"You must!" shrieked Aileen as she grabbed Janet's arm and yanked her away from the group.

In the blink of an eye, hell unleashed.

Men appeared. So many men, wearing the royal livery and armed with swords. Lachlan pulled Marjorie behind him and unsheathed his own sword, looking ready to slay each and every one, but the men stood shoulder to shoulder and continued to advance, trapping the two against a wooden fence.

Horror engulfed Janet like a sodden cloak, dark and suffocating. "Aileen. What have you *done*?"

"I did it for us," her former lover hissed. "A lady deserves so much better than the forced company of a traitor's daughter and a bastard knight. They shame you. And have betrayed your trust. Did you know they were seen marrying in this town? Against the queen's command? They are traitors! But do not worry; I shall protect you. Your very own Aileen, who loves you still. And you'll forget them soon enough."

Swallowing hard against the bile threatening to choke her, Janet shook her head. "No. *No.*"

But her words were swept away by the cool sea breeze. The townspeople had fled; the tradesmen and merchants cowered behind their stalls. No one would come to their aid. It would have to be her, and her alone.

"Sir Lachlan Ross!" bellowed one of the liveried strangers. "Lay down your sword in the name of Queen Margaret."

"No," snarled Lachlan. "I protect my own."

"Have a care for life and limb. You and Lady Marjorie Hepburn—"

"Ross," said Marjorie defiantly as she curled her hand around Lachlan's left arm. "My name is Lady Marjorie *Ross.*"

Ignoring her words, the young man instead unrolled a piece of parchment. "Sir Lachlan Ross. Lady Marjorie Hepburn. You stand accused of unlawful acts and offenses against the crown. You shall stand trial one week hence and until that time shall be confined to the dungeon below St. Andrews castle—"

Dungeon!

"They will not!" said Janet sharply as she wrenched away from the woman now her sworn enemy. For Aileen to conspire with the English-born queen, to commit such a heinous act of betrayal against Marjorie and Lachlan for her own selfish ends—unforgivable.

"Madam. I am ordered—"

"Do not dare *madam* me, laddie," snapped Janet, marching straight to him and poking his lean chest with one finger. "You know who I am?"

He gulped. "Aye, Lady Janet."

"Then you understand I have the king's ear, his great favor, and know his mind. Do you truly believe His Grace would permit his champion and his ward to be held in a dungeon?"

"Queen Margaret did so order," protested the young man weakly.

Janet itched to slap him a dozen times, to scream in her righteous fury and agonizing fear. But only a cool head, a steely spine, would win this day. "That may be how matters progress in *England*. Are you certain our enlightened, anointed *Scottish* sovereign is fully aware of the young queen's barbaric plan?"

"Uh…"

"Save your own neck, lad. Do not act in haste but confine the two so accused in chambers at my estate. There we can await the king's orders and ensure all due process for a *celebrated knight* and a *lady born*."

He turned to confer with his men, and Janet looked over at Lachlan and Marjorie, trying to convey without words her unwavering support, her affection, her determination to defy the devil-spawned Margaret Tudor until she drew her last breath.

After an eternity, the queen's man turned back. "Very well," he said grudgingly. "We'll send word to His Grace and await him at your estate. Any trouble, though, and it will be the dungeon for them both."

Marjorie trembled, but she raised her chin, and Lachlan inclined his head before turning and very deliberately kissing her on the lips, another defiance and the act of an unashamed and affectionate husband. Then, he slowly sheathed his sword.

Relief at the respite she'd gained nearly sent Janet to her knees, but she could not falter.

The sternest battle of her life lay ahead: defeat the queen and win freedom for her lovers or be defeated…and lose them forever.

Chapter Twelve

After weeks of freedom, to be imprisoned again was unbearable. Although saints and Janet be praised, she'd been confined the past two days to a comfortably furnished chamber rather than a dungeon.

A dungeon.

Marjorie pressed her knuckles to her lips to halt a wave of nausea. She might still be sent there if Queen Margaret had her way. The king's English wife was young, but she had a firm opinion on her superiority over anyone not of Tudor blood. She'd also already proven that she did not tolerate disobedience and would punish infractions in the harshest of ways.

Now, Marjorie's only hope, and indeed Lachlan's only hope—the brave, strong warrior who had sacrificed all to help her—was the king's prerogative of mercy. Which he might not be at all inclined to grant, considering she had wed without his permission and ruined a much-needed alliance with an English border lord.

A sharp trumpet blast clawed her already shredded

nerves, and she rushed to the window to see the king, queen, and a long retinue of others on horseback, plus several wagons, approach the manor.

The day of reckoning had arrived. And she had no idea what to do or what to say. Trays of food and watered wine had been delivered by stone-faced guards, but she'd been forbidden visitors. Although from raised voices outside her chamber she knew Janet had attempted to see both her and Lachlan, who had been confined to another chamber farther down the hallway.

Falling to her knees, Marjorie began to pray. For deliverance from this trial. To be reunited with her husband and mistress. To never set eyes on the queen again.

A thousand years later, the chamber door swung open and two stern-faced, silver-haired men in black robes appeared. One was tall and rounded, the other nearer to her own height and slender. Both had long silver-flecked beards, and the shorter man carried parchment, quill, and inkpot.

Somehow, she rose to her feet and curtsied. "Good afternoon, sirs."

"Lady Marjorie," said the taller man curtly. "I am Master Boyd; this is Master Douglas. We are legal clerks from Stirling, come to hear evidence on this grave matter and provide advice for judgment. We have spoken with Sir Lachlan; now we shall speak with you. Sit down, and we shall begin."

"Yes, sir," she replied, sinking onto a hard wooden chair. "My husband…he is well?"

"So," said Master Boyd, ignoring her question, "tell us in your own words the events leading to this day. Master Douglas shall act as scribe."

Marjorie swallowed hard. "I lived in a convent most of my life. Then I was summoned to Stirling Castle, where my guardian, His Grace the King, declared I would live with

Lady Janet Fraser, protected by Sir Lachlan Ross, until he decided on a husband for me. We traveled here by wagon—"

"A journey during which Sir Lachlan murdered four men, including Lord Kerr," said Master Douglas, his lip curling.

"No," she protested shakily. "He killed four men who fired arrows at the wagon and attempted to kidnap Lady Janet and myself. The king forgave the act."

"I see. Then what?"

"I was…we were…very content here. Guests came for supper one evening—"

"The Sinclairs and the Campbells," said Master Boyd, nodding. "Yes, we visited them on our way here. Sir Lachlan assaulted Angus Campbell, did he not?"

Marjorie's temper flared at the sneering tone. "Only because Angus accosted me in the garden!"

"It is Master Campbell's testimony that you welcomed his embrace, but when Sir Lachlan approached, you pretended not to so you might conceal your whorish nature."

Oh, how she wished she'd stabbed that rodent with her eating knife rather than deliver a mere foot stomp.

"Sir—"

"It was Master Campbell's concern you were being led astray that led him to send word to our good queen, who in her kindness and charity arranged a splendid match for you with an English baron. But you defied Her Grace," said Master Boyd, his black robe whipping about, his voice rising to a roar. "You, a lady born, thought to wed a bastard without permission and spat on the crown of Scotland, much like your traitor father!"

"No!"

Master Douglas shook his head. "Now is not the time for hysterics, Lady Marjorie. Only the truth."

"I speak the truth," she replied, gripping the folds of her gown so she might not stand and slap both men for the way they kept twisting her words. "And I have never, nor would ever, spit on the crown of Scotland. I love this land. I love my king."

Master Boyd glared at her. "Pretty words, lady. But I see only two possible truths. Either you were an innocent maiden, lured into a false marriage for coin by a sinful man forsaken by God…or you are a Jezebel who lured him to sin, deceived Lady Janet, and sought to defy our Queen Margaret for her own wicked ends. Which is it?"

Marjorie gritted her teeth to suppress a shriek of rage. Here it was, then. The offer. Betray Lachlan to these vile lawyers and be free or accept their destruction of her character. They were clearly the queen's men, emboldened by Angus Campbell's lies, and were angry they even had to speak to her for the show of a fair trial.

"Neither, sir," she replied unsteadily. "I wed a good, strong man for love. My marriage is not false. It is legal and proper, a promise signed and witnessed, if irregular in the eyes of the clergy. I am a wedded and, ah, bedded wife."

Master Douglas shuffled his pile of parchment before holding one page up. "This promise, signed and witnessed, given to me by Sir Lachlan?"

At the familiar document, the one signed by her and Lachlan, the St. Andrews lawyer Master Shaw, and his young clerk, Marjorie nodded eagerly. "Yes, sir."

"It looks fraudulent to me."

She froze. "Beg pardon?"

Master Boyd peered over the other man's shoulder and nodded. "Certainly fraudulent. Worthless to this case, I believe."

"Then there is only one thing to be done," said Master Douglas, smiling as he rose to his feet and walked toward the fireplace.

"Do not!" screamed Marjorie, but the man tossed the

copy of her marriage lines into the roaring fire as though it were an old rag. She stood, her chair clattering to the floor, and ran to him, only to be halted by Master Boyd's cruel grip around her upper arm.

"No," she whispered, dropping to her knees, as in moments the precious parchment was no more.

"As I said," mused Master Boyd, "there are only two possible truths for you. Innocent maiden lured into sin for her coin or lying, deceiving Jezebel with hatred in her heart for the king and queen. Choose wisely, dear lady. We shall see you soon in your trial. Good morrow."

Alone once more, Marjorie clasped her arms around herself, yet no tears fell in the fury and sick fear threatening to drown her. If the second copy Lachlan had given to Janet remained hidden, they had evidence still. If it had been found and burned, they had nothing but their word.

And she would be forced to publicly choose: betray Lachlan or accept filthy, near-treasonous lies about herself.

Indeed, no choice at all.

...

"More wine, lady?"

Janet took the full goblet from her servant with a grateful smile and nod. At least having something to occupy her hands, she wasn't so tempted to snatch bald the queen and all her ladies who were currently wandering the manor and cooing about its coziness and old-fashioned charm, as though she lived in a rustic pig pen. James stood by the window in the hall with several advisers, looking increasingly impatient and irritated.

If the situation weren't so dire and soul crushing, she might have reveled in her former lover's bad temper; the wretched man could have halted all this with a wave of his hand. Saints alive, she could think of several fair ladies who would happily leave the Highlands for an English title. Not to mention Lachlan's long and loyal service to the crown. But instead, James had indulged his queen in her fit of spite, and she did not admire him for it.

Janet took a sip of wine just for something to do. She hadn't slept in days but tossed and turned in worry for Marjorie and Lachlan. The devil-spawned guards had prevented her from seeing either, and her frustration and fury knew no bounds. Were they well? Had they been mistreated? The two lawyers from Stirling who had traveled ahead of the royal procession were about as distant from the learned, just, and delightfully irritable Master Shaw as it were possible to be. They cared less for the law and more for gaining favor with the queen. Which made them both dangerous indeed.

"Beg pardon," said another servant, a rotund young man who looked miserable rather than awed at being in the presence of the royal couple. "But His Grace has requested the hall be turned into a…ah…court. For the *trial* of Lady Marjorie and Sir Lachlan. How should it look? I do not know of such things. It is wrong. It is all wrong."

I could not agree more.

"Do not fret, lad. Fetch some others and move the dining table to the far wall. At the north end, set up a dais for the king and queen and the king's advisers. To the left, a table and chairs for the lawyers. To the right, a chair for whomever is being asked questions. Several benches with cushions for the queen's ladies. Can you remember all that?"

"Yes, my lady," he replied and dashed away.

Taking several calming breaths, Janet looked over again at the king. He met her gaze and smiled briefly but continued his conversation, and she barely stopped herself from hurling her goblet at his head for what he'd done and what he forced her to do this day.

Having Marjorie and Lachlan so close and yet not be allowed to see them, talk to them, touch them, was unbearable. All she'd been able to do to show her affection and support was personally oversee the dishes sent to their chambers, ensuring only the choicest cuts of meat, the freshest bread. Yes, back on the day Marjorie and Lachlan had been arrested, she'd sent word to Master Shaw, but she had no way of knowing if her letter had reached him or even if he would assist further.

In a battle directly with the queen, many men would not.

"Lady Janet."

She turned to see one of the king's many advisers, a harried-looking man with kind eyes that she did not personally know well. "Sir?"

"His Grace wishes the trial to begin shortly. He will hear the lawyers speak, then Lady Marjorie and Sir Lachlan. He also wishes to inform you that you are permitted to remain and observe proceedings but must sit with the queen's ladies. And, er, he said I must tell you to, er...*behave*."

Both annoyance and relief flooded her. "Please thank His Grace," she replied crisply. "And tell him I am, as ever, his loyal subject."

The man bowed, then bustled away.

Janet finished her wine and set the goblet down on the window ledge. Even holding something seemed too difficult, let alone an attempt to distract herself with embroidery or other task. Around her, the hall was being transformed into a small court, and it made her ill. Yes, soon she would see Marjorie and Lachlan, but equally as soon, their trial would begin.

Had she done enough to help them? Would she be the reason one or both were imprisoned or worse? It had been her idea for them to marry in the irregular way, after all. And that shocking arrest at the market happened before she had the chance to explain fully about Aileen, that she no longer loved the woman. That instead they were the ones who held a place in her heart.

Janet rubbed a weary hand over her face. If James ceased being a coward in his avoidance of her, she could have pleaded the case of her two lovers. Explained her role in the matter. Promised the moon, the sun, and the stars if he would just grant them mercy and bring this nightmare to an end.

But he had denied her that chance. It might be that her time in favor had come to a close, and she was indeed destined to lose everyone and everything she cared about.

A truly chilling thought when she had already lost so much.

"Lady Janet?" called one of the queen's English ladies impatiently. "Do sit down. They are ready to begin."

Clasping her hands in a futile effort at tranquility, she sat at the end of the second bench for the queen's ladies. The last thing she wanted was to be trapped within a chirping circle of Englishwomen who thought this entertaining. At the far end of the hall, James and Margaret sat on a raised dais; he still looked supremely irritated, but she looked both smug and excited. The lawyers took their seats, and then the guard at the door thumped a wooden staff on the floor and announced, "Lady Marjorie Hepburn. Sir Lachlan Ross."

Her heart in her mouth, Janet leaned forward.

Marjorie entered with an armed escort first. Her shoulders were back, her chin high, but her face looked deathly pale and her eyes a little swollen.

Staring helplessly, furious she could not do more, Janet managed to meet her gaze, touching two fingers to her lips in a discreet half kiss, and her former ward smiled a little. Then Lachlan entered the hall, surrounded by men at least a head shorter and appearing even more irritated than the king. When he saw Marjorie remained unharmed, his shoulders relaxed, and when Janet met his gaze and sent him his half kiss, he inclined his head and placed a hand over his heart.

So courtly.

A sob lodged in her throat.

Yes, my pet, I am impressed.

James clapped his hands together and stood. "Queen Margaret. Lords and ladies. Learned men of the law and clergy. We are here to determine a matter concerning my ward Lady Marjorie Hepburn and my champion Sir Lachlan Ross. I will hear facts and honest opinion. I will not permit a *spectacle*. Do so proceed, Master Boyd."

The lawyer stood and doffed his cap. "Your Graces. Learned friends. We are here to examine grave offenses against the crown, committed by the man and woman so accused..."

Janet twisted her fingers together.

The reckoning had begun.

. . .

Once, he'd had the greatest respect for learned men. But in one day, Boyd and Douglas had turned his good opinion forever.

Lachlan watched in enraged silence as the lawyers smiled. As they paced. As they gestured.

As they lied.

The things they'd said in this hall to Marjorie, the half truths and twisting of her words, the "evidence" from Angus Campbell and Aileen Campbell. Sneering comments about his humble illegitimate birth. His "murder" of the four men who had attacked the wagon and threatened the ladies.

And through it all, James said nothing, just sat in brooding silence. If it weren't for Lady Janet, his steadfast mistress, he might have thought he'd been forsaken entirely.

But he hadn't been. Nor had Marjorie. They might not have seen Lady Janet for days, nor had she spoken of love, but her deeds spoke for her. In truth, deeds were far more reassuring. The two lawyers had just proven how false and worthless words could be.

"A-hem! Sir Lachlan. Please *do* favor the court with an answer to the question," said Master Douglas, his words near dripping with disdain.

Plague take it. Which one now? It seemed as though the smiling viper had fired a thousand poisoned arrows, and he could scarcely think anymore. "C-could you r-repeat it?"

"Beg pardon, sir?"

Lachlan gritted his teeth at the overloud tone, the sly looks, the muffled laughs and whispers behind hands at his faltering speech. "I…ah…asked…"

"Sir Lachlan requested that the question be repeated, Master Douglas," the king said crisply. "Listen more closely."

The lawyer blinked and mopped his brow with a linen square. "Yes, Your Grace. Sir Lachlan, on the twentieth day of July, Lady Janet received a missive from our good queen. Did she inform you of the contents?"

"Aye."

"And what did it say?"

"You know…what it s-said."

Master Douglas gave him a pitying look, as though he were a witless child. No doubt in the courtroom he was. But with a longsword or other weapon, he would best the lawyer with one hand tied behind his back. "Please, Sir Lachlan. For the court—"

James clapped his hands once. "The letter said Her Grace the queen had arranged a marriage for Lady Marjorie to an English baron in Carlisle two weeks hence. Master Douglas, as you seem to be struggling with the art of questioning a witness, and for the sake of brevity, I ask you to sit and allow your learned friend to continue."

Master Boyd rose to his feet and replaced his red-faced friend. "Sir Lachlan. Pray tell, how did the household react to the letter, and what did you do next?"

Lachlan scowled at the memory of Marjorie's tears, of Lady Janet's worried pacing as she thought of a plan. For that injustice, for the love he bore the two women in his life, both strong in their own way, both courageous in overcoming adversity…he would force his wretched mouth to work. He would make these lawyers and all the people present understand. "Distress. As Lady Marjorie said…she did not want…to marry an Englishman. So I offered. To wed her."

"For coin?"

"No," he snarled.

"Come now, sir, there is no shame in coin changing hands. You are a man of little means. Surely you must have expected payment for so great a burden in defying an order of our good queen. And Lady Marjorie is an heiress."

"No."

Master Boyd laughed. "So you chose to commit a terrible act…for *nothing*?"

"Not for nothing. Because I cared. Because it was right. Because she is…a good woman. The very best."

"How interesting. But you knew it was terrible, for you rode away with Lady Marjorie to St. Andrews without informing the guards. Did you inform Lady Janet?"

"Lady Janet was…in the chapel," he replied. The lawyers were not the only ones who could speak a half truth. "Praying."

"I see. But this next part is where it becomes…unclear. You claim to have wed Lady Marjorie in an irregular ceremony, with a written promise, witnessed and signed by a Master Shaw and his clerk."

A chill prickled the back of Lachlan's neck. "What is

unclear?"

"My learned friend and I searched and searched, but we could not find either this Master Shaw or his clerk. Nor can you produce any evidence of this promise—"

"I gave you…the d-document."

Master Boyd shook his head sadly. "No, sir, you did not. I can only conclude that this tale of a marriage is false and fraudulent and that Lady Marjorie is in fact free to wed as Her Grace the queen so arranged."

The room erupted. Queen Margaret clapped her hands in delight, and James sat forward in his chair, his brow creasing. His advisers offered loud opinions among themselves, and the queen's ladies whispered and giggled. Stunned at the bold lie from a man supposedly here to uphold the law, Lachlan glanced at Marjorie. Very deliberately, she tilted her head toward the hall fireplace, and understanding dawned. *Burned.* The vermin had burned his copy of the marriage promise.

Did they find the second copy?

"Silence," snapped the king. "If there are no witnesses and no document, I can only rule in one way…"

Master Boyd bowed. "Your Grace—"

"Unless of course there is anyone else present with evidence relevant to this matter?"

Lachlan held his breath, not daring to look at his mistress. And then he heard the sweetest words in history. Bold and clear for everyone in the hall to hear.

"I have such evidence, Your Grace. If I may humbly approach."

James nodded. "You may, Lady Janet."

Lachlan could only gaze in awe as she marched toward the dais, a beautiful, wise termagant about to unleash hell. The room erupted again when she reached into the bodice of her gown to retrieve a folded piece of parchment and handed it to the king, and Lachlan pressed a fist to his lips so he did not laugh at the horror on the lawyer's face, the anger on Queen Margaret's, or how perfectly Janet Fraser it was to conceal an important document in such a place.

God's blood, how he loved her.

"Hmm," said James eventually. "I hold in my hand a document that I have examined and find to be proper and legal. It is a marriage promise between Lady Marjorie Hepburn and Sir Lachlan Ross, signed and witnessed. I declare it valid. However…"

The hall went so quiet they could have heard a mouse breathe, and Lachlan gripped his thighs. What now?

"However," the king continued, "it is not right or proper that Her Grace the queen's orders were disobeyed. The queen's command is as my command; therefore punishment is required for the wrongdoing. Sir Lachlan Ross, Lady Marjorie Ross, stand together and be sentenced."

Silently Lachlan rose to his feet before walking to Marjorie. She took his arm, and he covered her hand with his and squeezed it because she was his cherished wedded wife, and woe betide anyone who attempted to come between them. Whatever the punishment, they would face it together. "Your Grace?"

James had never looked sterner. "I am imposing a substantial fine. Sir Lachlan and Lady Marjorie, you shall both forfeit all property and coin. It is only my love for you that you do not forfeit your freedom. Be wed but destitute from this day…unless offered shelter, of course."

"I do so offer," announced Lady Janet. "If Your Grace will permit."

"Granted. Now this matter is concluded; the legal minds shall depart. Lady Janet, you will offer Highland hospitality for the evening to your king, queen, and the court, yes?"

She curtsied. "As Your Grace wishes."

Still reeling at the verdict, unable to say a word, Lachlan curved an arm around Marjorie's shoulders. With a choked cry, she flung herself against him, and he held her tightly before leaning down and kissing her thoroughly. Saying with his lips what his mouth could not.

All that they needed now was Lady Janet with them to be complete, and when he glanced up and met his mistress's soft gaze, she smiled.

"Take your wife to the solar, Sir Lachlan. I shall join you there presently."

His breath caught.

At last, it seemed, paradise might just be possible.

Chapter Thirteen

"Now, Jannie. You do understand it would be a treasonous act to hurl that goblet at my head?"

Janet took a long swallow of wine, then saluted James with her weapon of choice. "While the thought of a goblet-shaped imprint on your forehead brings me great satisfaction, it would be a shameful waste of good wine, Your Grace."

The king's lips twitched as he leaned against the chapel's inner wall. "With your aim, I must declare you a low threat to my royal person."

"Maybe my aim has improved," she replied archly.

"Unwary guards shall rejoice to hear it."

Janet didn't laugh. "How could you, James?" she asked softly. "How could you do that to Lachlan? To me? What you put us and dear Marjorie through is quite unforgivable."

He rubbed a hand over his face, and just for a moment she saw a man weighed down with a thousand cares. "In the morning I leave for the border. There are strong rumors of an uprising, and I must quell it. Another noble English and Scottish alliance by marriage would have been helpful... I did not want this trial, Jannie. But if Margaret had complained to her father, to diplomats and dignitaries, that she had been slighted, the English would have seized upon the excuse to make trouble. I do not wish for war with them or border raids; I have enough cares already in trying to hold this realm together. To stop my own clans and nobles warring and raiding. To replenish the treasury."

"You walk along a cliff edge," she admitted.

"Every hour of every day. However, trust that I always knew how the play would end. Because you are a clever lass, you had two copies of the promise made and argued those guards away from use of a dungeon. Now that is legal cunning. But I do know where Master Shaw and his clerk are, and if that document wasn't stuffed in your *bodice*, then they would have appeared as witnesses. Queen Margaret will learn in time she resides in Scotland, and her bullish, arrogant Tudor ways are unwelcome here. But for better or worse, she is my wife and must be given all due respect."

Janet nodded reluctantly. "I understand your decision. I like it not, for it hurt me and those I love, but I do understand."

"Oh, you love them, do you?" said James softly, his lips curling into a self-satisfied smirk.

She froze. And yet the astonishing words had come out of her mouth. "I...er..."

"Oh-ho! No retreating now, my fiery lass. In truth I gifted you Lachlan because I thought you might do well together. He needs a strong lady, and there is none more so than you. Never did I think you would open your heart to him *and* Lady Marjorie. But you have always been a woman who forged her own path."

"Who says I have opened my heart to anyone?" she bit out, boldly dissembling to her king when that was exactly what had happened, even after swearing she would never love again after Fergus.

James smiled, a little too morosely for her liking. "Go to them, Jannie. Declare yourself. You know as well as I do that happiness can be snatched away in a heartbeat, the one you love gone from you in an instant due to illness, nefarious actions, or an accident. Revel in every moment you have. Go now. I will act as host, as I have done so many times in this house."

She ran to him, kissing his cheek and embracing him tightly. "Stay safe. Scotland needs you, Your Grace, for a very long reign. You will always be dear to my heart."

"God bless and keep you, beloved."

With one last deep curtsy to her king, Janet turned and departed the chapel, nearly stumbling on the stairs in her haste to get to the solar where Lachlan and Marjorie waited. And yet when she reached the door, her steps halted.

For a woman who had fought so hard and so long to establish command, choosing to be vulnerable again was an unnerving thing. The notion did not sit at all easily on her shoulders, and here she was about to offer her heart into the safekeeping of not one but *two* people. Love carried great risk, even more so as a trio, and the likelihood of her making mistakes as she'd done, of closing herself away from the chaotic nature of emotion was high.

And yet...love brought joy. Comfort and understanding. The promise of a better and brighter tomorrow.

She wanted that in her life. *Needed* it.

Taking a deep breath, Janet pushed open the solar door before latching it behind her. In the center of the room, seated on the chaise, were Marjorie and Lachlan.

Both rose to their feet, Lachlan bowing and Marjorie curtsying.

"So," said Janet, inwardly cursing as a boulder lodged in her throat. "Here we are."

"Lady..." said Lachlan hoarsely. "*Mistress.*"

Wordlessly, she held out her arms, and soon she was whole again as they embraced, her body rejoicing at the sensation of Lachlan's brute strength and Marjorie's plump curves pressed against it.

"My pet," she whispered, kissing Lachlan square on the mouth before turning to Marjorie and doing the same. "My dear one. I was so afraid this might end differently. So very afraid. To lose you both would have been…"

Marjorie shuddered. "I cannot bear to think about it. When that vile lawyer burned the copy of the promise in front of me, I despaired that he might have found your copy and done the same. But it was in your bodice!"

A soft laugh escaped. "I tucked it there when I saw the lawyers arrive. They did in fact search my chamber. I wish them to purgatory for what they did."

"You were so steadfast," said Lachlan. "You and Marjorie. No forsaking. No betrayal. Even when…they offered temptation."

Janet raised an imperious brow. "They could have offered all the gold in Scotland, and I would not break. Some things…some things are so precious they must be fought for until your last breath."

"Such as?" said Marjorie, her gaze intent, her smile hopeful.

"Come with me. To the chaise," she replied, guiding both until they settled on either side of her on the sturdy piece of furniture. Ensuring all hands were clasped, she took another deep breath to prepare for the most important declaration of her life. "I did not think to love again. I thought my heart died with Fergus and that I would be content with affairs where they did not truly know me. I did not *want* them to know me, for when another knows your true self, they have great power. But then the king gifted me a Highland Beast and a convent virgin, and my entire world turned upside down. I began to *feel* again. I liked it not."

"And now?" Lachlan rasped.

Janet shifted on the chaise. Devil take it, words were difficult when she would much rather show them with acts. "Now…it seems my world can only be complete with both a man and a woman to love. To protect. To cherish and command. No other man but Sir Lachlan Ross and no other woman but Lady Marjorie Ross will do. And that is that. I love you both. For always."

Silence greeted her words, and Janet tensed. Then Marjorie burst into tears and cuddled closer, and Lachlan moved to kneel at her feet, and a flame lit inside her. A flame that no trial or burden or unspoken words could douse.

Joy. At long last.

. . .

Lady Janet loved them.

Staring up at his two women, Lachlan drank in the perfection of the moment. Their clasped hands. Lady Janet's smile. Marjorie's tears of happiness.

After the trial, when he and Marjorie had sat on the chaise, waiting for their mistress, they'd both been too weary, too emptied by the events of the previous days, to do more than just lean against each other, heads touching and fingers linked. Each taking comfort in the other, each waiting for the fiery redhead needed to make their world and marriage complete. The wait had seemed forever as he stared at the door, his ears straining for the sound of footsteps on the stairs, tormented by an agony of hope. For justice to be served, the king had taken everything he and Marjorie possessed, except their marriage. Lady Janet had offered shelter, and he yearned for that to mean so much more than charity.

What she'd just declared had been beyond his wildest

dreams.

Lady Janet loved them.

Lachlan swallowed hard. "I am s-so…h-h…"

He cursed as a rush of emotion tangled his tongue and robbed him of speech. He wanted to say the words. Needed to say them after holding them inside for so long.

Lady Janet let go of his hand and instead leaned forward and cupped his cheek. "Yes, my pet?"

"Take your time, Lachlan," said Marjorie, beaming at him. "We have all the time in the world now."

Lifting her hand to his lips, he kissed it swiftly. Then he rubbed his cheek against Lady Janet's hand, more Beast than ever before in the desire for affection. Now he'd had the taste of what it meant as a grown man to be loved, to be cared for, he could stand in the shadows no more.

"I am," he began, using all his will to get the words out in a clear manner, "so *happy*. Lady Janet…I have loved you… so long. To hear you…love me in return…is…is…a miracle. I had stopped…b-believing. My face. My body. My *speech*. I thought to n-never…find love. Then I was…blessed *twice*. A beloved mistress…and a beloved wife. Marjorie…"

"Aye, husband?" she asked, her smile turning impish.

"I fought…what I felt…for you. How could I c-care for… how could I love…*two* women? Two women…so different? But n-now I understand. *All* my needs met. To kneel. To protect and serve. A woman to…command me. A woman to…soothe me. And it is…*paradise*."

"It is, rather," said Lady Janet. "Marjorie? Do you wish to say anything, dear one?"

His wife nodded, squeezing both their hands. "My whole life, I was forsaken. Because of what my father did, I thought the most I could hope for was an ancient husband who might be kind. Never did I think I would meet a bold, beautiful, learned *woman* I desired. How could something called sinful feel so right? But then came more. A man I desired also. And this strong, brave man wed me. The desire soon blossomed into love. But although I hoped and prayed, I did not think to have that love returned, for surely I would never be good enough for the great Lady Janet Fraser or the great Sir Lachlan Ross. Yet...with your love, your teaching, your protection, I...I found myself at last. I found my voice and my purpose. I found courage to face the new and dangerous and unexpected. I found I am worthy. And for that, you have my loyalty and devotion. For always."

"Perfectly said," replied Lady Janet, turning to kiss Marjorie sweetly on the lips.

Utterly content, Lachlan leaned forward and rested his head on Lady Janet's lap, his arms stretching to curve around each lady's outer thigh. When two hands began stroking his hair, he thought he might happily stay like this forever.

Until those two hands tangled in his hair and roughly tugged his head up.

Sucking in a harsh breath at the delicious prickle of pain, Lachlan stared up at the two women, who were looking back at him with *very* wicked smiles.

"We've each declared our hearts," said Lady Janet. "Now it is time to show that love with our bodies."

"Ooooh, yes," said Marjorie, her eyes sparkling. "Touching myself is quite wonderful, but it cannot compare to being touched and kissed and fucked by you both."

Lachlan laughed, delighted at her candor. She had been well taught. "What do my ladies w-wish?"

"On your feet, pet," said Lady Janet. "Marjorie and I shall assist you in undressing."

Even the thought of their hands on him once more almost made him moan. Never had he scrambled to his feet so swiftly.

His women teased him unmercifully as they slowly

removed his mantle, then unhooked the fastenings on his doublet, rubbing their breasts against his chest and back and arms, their fingers brushing his swelling cock and the curve of his arse through his hose.

Marjorie paused and tilted her head. "May I ask…why always a red doublet?"

Lachlan smiled ruefully. "The color was…my mother's favorite. Naught to do with…blood."

"We shall conceal that fact from your enemies," said Lady Janet, her eyes glinting. "Now for that shirt. 'Tis a sin to keep that magnificent chest covered."

Soon soft fingers caressed his skin, threaded through his chest hair, and tweaked his nipples before moving down to strip him of his shoes, hose, and stockings. By the time he stood naked, he panted with need.

"Now, pet," purred Lady Janet. "We are going to undress dear Marjorie. Tease her until she needs sweet release as much as you do."

His heart pounding with excitement, Lachlan assisted his mistress with undressing his wife. First her hood, then girdle and silver-embroidered gown, kirtle, and finally her shift, shoes, and stockings. Unable to resist the temptation, he stood behind Marjorie and cupped her breasts in his hands, pinching her tender nipples before offering them to Lady Janet to be sucked.

Marjorie whimpered.

"Something the matter, dear one?" asked Lady Janet lazily, flicking her tongue over those swollen tips as one finger trailed down Marjorie's stomach, parted her bush, and stroked her center.

"Is she wet enough, mistress?" Lachlan rasped, gently biting the curve of his wife's neck and turning her whimpers into a pleading cry.

"Not quite, pet. Sit on the chaise with Marjorie on your

lap. Spread her thighs wide for me. You want me to taste that sweet little cunt, don't you dear one?"

"Please," Marjorie begged. "*Please*."

Almost shaking with lust, his cock throbbing with the need to spend, Lachlan sat on the chaise and carefully settled his wife on his lap, hooking her legs over his before sliding both hands down and parting the crisp hair. Marjorie's hips circled in an attempt to get him to touch her pearl, but his questing fingers merely circled the swollen bud before delving farther down to stroke the pink, petal-soft flesh. Already the heady scent of her arousal perfumed the air.

Lady Janet licked her lips, her gaze pure hunger, and Lachlan grinned.

"Enjoy your feast, mistress."

"Oh, I shall."

• • •

Lachlan's brawny chest supporting her, Janet's wicked tongue teasing her, was wondrous enough. But knowing they both loved her also...

Marjorie trembled, her heart so full, her body craving the touch of her husband and mistress so much, she could scarcely see straight. Each time they were together, she thought she knew how pleasure felt and what to expect. Yet each time Janet and Lachlan took her to new heights, and now, safe and loved and cherished and protected, it seemed she might soar to the heavens. Just a moment more. A moment more of Lachlan kissing and nipping at her neck, and Janet sucking her pearl and gently penetrating her with two fingers, and she would reach an ecstasy like no other...

Her eyes flew open. "Nooooo!" she spluttered. "Why did you stop?"

Janet sat back on her heels and licked her glistening lips.

"Because, dear one, we are going to change position. I shall undress, then we'll arrange some cushions on the ground for Lachlan to lie on. While you ride him until he spends every drop of seed inside you, he will lick my cunt."

Marjorie stilled, hardly daring to hope, and below her, she felt Lachlan tense in surprise also. "Inside me?"

"Well, it is the most successful way of trying for a child."

"Are you sure?" asked Lachlan. "That will be…hurtful for you."

Janet took a deep breath. "I wish only for your happiness. I understand it is a child that will make you happy, and you have my blessing. Yes, if you succeed I will be joyful, but there will be days that hurt. When I am envious and sad, disappointed and angry that my body always failed me in this one task. On those days I will need special care. Patience and compassion and reassurance that I have much to offer this trio."

"But you do!" burst out Marjorie. "You are the fire that sparks us. The armor that protects. The wise woman who lovingly nurtures."

"*Nurture?*" her mistress looked at her, brow furrowed. "Me? How can you say that when I prefer someone else coddles and comforts the upsets?"

Lachlan cleared his throat. "Not all show love…the same way. Some do with words. Others with touch. But commanders show they c-care…with *acts*. When they lead. When they resolve. When they teach. When they guide others…safely home. A child needs words. Touch. And acts. They will need *you*. As we do."

"Always," said Marjorie.

"Well," said Janet, her eyes overbright. "*Well*."

"May I undress you, mistress?"

"You may."

Sliding from Lachlan's lap—unable to halt a whimper

when the movement sent a jolt to her aching, burning center—Marjorie helped Janet remove her hood, girdle, and scarlet gown, then kirtle and shift, shoes and stockings. For a moment she allowed herself the pleasure of just gazing on Janet's beautiful body, the long sleek limbs, those sweet pale-brown nipples, the tight red curls that covered her mound.

"The way you two look at me," said Janet softly, "is quite something. As though I am the most beautiful woman in the world, and you cannot wait to worship me. Is that blasphemous?"

"Nay. Only truth," said Lachlan, taking his engorged cock in hand and rubbing it absently.

Marjorie squeezed her thighs together, aching for the moment she would be stuffed full. For this time, there would be no anxiety of the unknown, no pinch of pain, only pure pleasure.

Janet laughed. "Then let it be known that I am ready and quite, quite willing to be worshipped by you both."

"If you insist," he replied, his eyes glinting before arranging several large cushions on the floor to sit on and resting his head on the chaise.

Going up on her toes, Marjorie kissed Janet, sighing in delight when her mistress returned it in full measure, all demanding lips and darting tongue. She could taste a little of her own musky honey, and anticipation swept through her.

Pleasure, together. A child…together.

Wetter than she'd ever been, Marjorie dropped to her knees and crawled to Lachlan. He nodded his permission, his gaze almost black with lust as she took his thick cock in her hands and gently caressed it before flicking the swollen head with just the tip of her tongue, back and forth until she had the taste of him in her mouth. Then, she straddled his thighs and guided his cock to her entrance, dampening him further with her own honey as her greedy cunt welcomed him inside.

They both moaned.

Nimble as a cat, Janet arranged herself to be pleasured with both feet on the floor, her cunt above Lachlan's face, and her arms braced behind her on the chaise. When she teased him with her bush, Lachlan growled, his chin jerking in an attempt to reach the concealed treat. But today their mistress was in a benevolent mood, and she soon lowered herself enough so he could penetrate her with his tongue.

Marjorie had never seen anything so erotic.

"Ride him, dear one," commanded Janet, her eyes growing heavy lidded as Lachlan plundered her cunt, his big hands gripping her thighs. "Master that thick cock. And touch your pearl. I want to watch you pleasure yourself. It is one of my favorite things."

Using Lachlan's chest and her knees for leverage, Marjorie began to move. The sensation of fullness and his cock throbbing inside her made her gasp, but when her inner walls clamped around him and he bucked, she fully understood her sensual power. Then, as her eyes darted between Janet's avid gaze and the heady sight of Lachlan feasting, Marjorie slid her free hand between her legs, teasing her pearl as she circled her hips. But soon, far too soon, the urgent need for release overwhelmed her, and she moved faster and faster, rising and falling on her husband's cock, her fingertips frantically rubbing her swollen pearl.

Janet's head fell back, and as she ground her cunt against Lachlan's face, a low scream tore from her throat. Such a beautifully uninhibited sight sent Marjorie over the edge, and a moment later her world splintered, hurling her into a perfect storm of acute pleasure. Her cry echoed around the solar, her release only strengthened when Lachlan's hips bucked again, ramming his cock deep inside her and flooding her with hot seed.

When she at last returned to her senses, Marjorie found

herself cradled against Lachlan's chest, his arm curved around her waist. Janet lay on her side next to her, rearranging cushions, freeing trapped locks of hair, and wiping Lachlan's face clean with the hem of her shift.

Marjorie tried to move, but she was so warm and comfortable it was a half-hearted attempt at best. "Forgive me, Lachlan," she mumbled. "Limbs disobeying."

A laugh rumbled in his chest. "I shall survive."

"I hope so," said Janet. "We have many more positions to try. I'm quite certain one of them will result in Marjorie conceiving a child."

Marjorie reached out and linked her fingers with Janet's. "I love you. So very much. And you, Lachlan, my man pillow."

"Pleased to be…of service. To my ladies."

Janet smiled. "I've decided we're going to live boldly, scandalously, and very happily ever after."

Marjorie nodded, her heart overflowing with bliss. "Yes, mistress."

Epilogue

St. Andrews, September 1504

"Wine. Did I order enough wine? And where is that fishmonger? I made it plain I would tolerate no mischief when it came to delivery. At least the butcher is reliable. It only took two gentle reminders for him to realize he must provide the finest cuts of beef and lamb within the day..."

Stifling a grin, Janet watched Marjorie pace the larder, requiring no other body for her conversation. At her side paced Belle, the one-eyed kitchen pup of unknown breeds who had followed Marjorie home from the market a month prior, decided to stay, and nipped backsides on command. The way her lover had blossomed with the responsibility of managing the household delighted her to no end. Marjorie reveled in her tasks and had the merchants in town dancing to her tune.

"A short walk, dear one? It is a little overwarm in here."

Marjorie huffed out a breath. "We have a great deal to prepare for the banquet tonight. Guests are coming from as far as Edinburgh. You said a small gathering of like-minded souls, but it's nearly half the court!"

"You love it."

Smiling sheepishly, Marjorie nodded. "I do. I just feel so useful. And accomplished."

For the moment they were alone, so Janet kissed her. "Because you are. My ladies banquets shall become renowned. Both for the food and wine, and the blunt, detailed bedchamber advice given afterward. As the worst sinner in Scotland, I feel eminently qualified to provide such important knowledge."

"Worst sinner? Or legendary lady of lust?"

Janet nodded thoughtfully and tucked Marjorie's arm through hers, deliberately brushing her breast and making her quiver. "I may be introduced just so from this day forward. Now, let us go and watch Lachlan train. He should be sufficiently sweat-dampened."

"Some air would be welcome," admitted Marjorie as they left the larder and made their way outdoors to the courtyard. "One of the chefs is preparing a mushroom sauce, and the scent I once loved is now turning my stomach. I dare not tell Lachlan; he'll probably toss the man into a prickly hedgerow. This morning he threatened to tie me to the bed if I did not rest. By the saints, I've only missed one bleed. We do not know for sure."

"I fear our Beast will become quite unbearable if you are with child. I may have to tie *him* to the bed. And administer a gag."

"I do not believe he would consider that a punishment, mistress."

"Oh, I'm sure we could make it so," said Janet with a wink, and Marjorie laughed.

After the heat of the kitchens, the cool autumn air refreshed her face, although she was glad of her cloak. It could get very windy in St. Andrews. Fortunately the makeshift battlefield Lachlan had constructed to train young lads for future service to the king was mostly protected by the stables to one side and a solid hedgerow on the other.

"He's a good teacher," said Marjorie as they approached the roped-off area. Several lads waited in a line with swords in hand for their turn, all watching Lachlan correct the stance and grip of those in another small group. "So patient."

"There is no better than the king's champion. And with the school under royal warrant, James will have properly trained men when he needs to summon an army. Even with an English-born queen, I think there will always be tensions."

Both women sighed a little when Lachlan began demonstrating advance and retreat. The way he *moved*. Deadly, precise, ruthless, and yet so graceful, as though the longsword was part of him, an extension of his brawny arms. More than a few cocky young ones had found themselves sprawled on the ground, a sword tip to the throat, when they'd made the grave mistake of thinking Lachlan's enormous size or his age meant he would be slow or ungainly.

"Ladies," Lachlan hailed, and after pairing the lads off to practice, he walked over to where they stood.

Janet smiled, making an effort to not lick her lips at how deliciously rumpled and manly he looked. "Marjorie and I did not mean to interrupt. We just wished to admire you raising a sweat."

"They are a mixed g-group of lads," said Lachlan, wiping his brow with a cool cloth. "Some very good. Some terrible."

Janet and Marjorie exchanged smirks.

"Yes," said Marjorie. "*Lads.*"

"Far more accurate to say nine lads and one lass," said Janet wryly.

His jaw dropped. "You know?"

She rolled her eyes. "I have known Lady Isla Sutherland

since her birth. Why she wants to wear a wig, bind her breasts, and handle swords is her own business, but I'm quite sure her cold and falsely virtuous parents have no idea of this particular pastime."

"It's not right," Lachlan grumbled. "Lady with a longsword. I should…send her away."

"Why don't you, then?" asked Marjorie, her eyes glinting.

Lachlan scowled, and both ladies burst out laughing. They all knew full well it would do no good. From her first lesson, it had been clear Isla was unusually talented, spirited, and stubborn as an ornery goat. Sometimes she fell down, but she always got up, watched Lachlan intently, mimicked his actions, and demanded further tutoring. If he sent her away, Isla would no doubt change her clothes and wig and march straight back. Highland lasses were indeed a law unto themselves. Besides, when she mastered a skill, Lachlan preened unashamedly afterward. He would be the most wonderful father.

"Will this lesson go for much longer, pet?" asked Janet.

"Not very," said Lachlan, his expression turning hopeful. "You need me?"

"Always," said Marjorie.

He placed his hand over his heart and inclined his head, his gaze hot and loving, just the way they liked it. "Then I shall j-join you soon. In the solar?"

"Aye," said Janet demurely. "We'll be on the chaise… embroidering."

"I adore embroidering," added Marjorie. "For hours and hours."

Lachlan near galloped back to his students, and Janet and Marjorie linked arms and turned to walk back to the manor.

A man *and* a woman to love. All with tasks that delighted and fulfilled.

Life was indeed paradise.

Acknowledgments

I am grateful to many people who helped bring Scandalous Passions to life. My CP, Sherilee Gray, for her longstanding support and encouragement in writing the erotic books of my heart, especially the queer ones. Those in the Wicked Wallflowers Coven and on social media, whose cheerleading and many kindnesses keep me going. My readers—you are the very best. Those excited emails, messages, and tweets mean the world. And my editor, Lydia Sharp: thank you for championing this book and offering constructive guidance plus all the smiley faces an author could want.

I consulted the following in my research:
Scotland: A Concise History by Fitzroy Maclean
The Illustrated Encyclopedia of Royal Britain by Charles Phillips
Corsets and Codpieces: A Social History of Outrageous Fashion by Karen Bowman
A History of Scotland by Neil Oliver
*Margaret Tudor, Queen of Scots: The Life of King Henry

VIII's Sister by Sarah-Beth Watkins

"In all gudly haste": The Formation of Marriage in Scotland, c. 1350-1600 by Heather Parker

'Origins and Development of St. Andrews' in *St. Andrews Conservation Area Appraisal and Management Plan* by Fife Council

The Online Etymology Dictionary

Mister Slang's Timelines of Slang (Jonathon Green)

www.stirlingcastle.scot

www.undiscoveredscotland.co.uk/stirling/stirlingcastle

About the Author

New Zealander Nicola Davidson always adored words, romance and history, so writing historical romance was a logical career progression…er, eventually. After completing a communications degree and journalism diploma she left to teach English in Taiwan and travel through Asia before returning home to work in television. Jobs in tertiary education, local government communications and print media followed, but the lords and ladies in her head wouldn't hold their peace a moment longer and so began the years of professional daydreaming. When not chained to a computer writing wickedly sexy, witty and twisty turny stories, Nicola can be found ambling along a beach, cheering on the champion All Blacks rugby team or driving her nearest and dearest batty with her history geekisms, chocolate hoarding and complete lack of domestic skills.

Also by Nicola Davidson

HIS FORBIDDEN LADY

ONE FORBIDDEN KNIGHT

The Fallen Series

SURRENDER TO SIN

THE DEVIL'S SUBMISSION

THE SEDUCTION OF VISCOUNT VICE

If you love erotica, one-click these hot Scorched titles…

THE SCANDALOUS DIARY OF LILY LAYTON
a *Sweetest Taboo* novel by Stacy Reid

Oliver Carlyle, Marquess of Ambrose, has finally found the perfect wife, a woman who will not hide from his dark, carnal cravings. He just needs to figure out who she is. When he has a secret rendezvous with a mysterious stranger, suddenly he starts to believe *she* might be the author of the scandalous diary he discovered. His biggest fear—and deepest fantasy—is she may be the one woman he cannot have.

WILLFUL DEPRAVITY
a novel by Ingrid Hahn

The Marquess of Ashcroft was born to do two things. Paint and rut. The moment he sees Miss Patience Emery he knows he must have her for both. Patience is a large woman who has resigned herself to having a man only in her dreams. But when Lord Ashcroft approaches her with a chance to act on her bold, scandalous, and depraved desires, she sees her opportunity to indulge in every wicked fantasy she's ever had…

TWO DUKES AND A LADY
a novel by Lorna James

Dukes Charles Ashdown and William Kenwood love womanizing too much to ever be ensnared by a debutante. Certainly, no decent wife would allow their debauchery. But the only woman they've ever loved is back. After her husband's mysterious death, Lillian Drew finds solace with her girlhood crushes, Charles and William. When her dead husband's creditors hound her, she has no choice but to remarry, though she can't make up her mind which duke she'll propose to.

Made in the USA
Middletown, DE
27 June 2021